ROWAN THE DREAMWEAVER

Suzanne Stewart

SilverWood

Published in 2021 by SilverWood Books

SilverWood Books Ltd
14 Small Street, Bristol, BS1 1DE, United Kingdom
www.silverwoodbooks.co.uk

ISBN 978-1-80042-151-6 (paperback)
ISBN 978-1-80042-184-4 (ebook)

British Library Cataloguing in Publication Data
A CIP catalogue record for this book is
available from the British Library

Page design and typesetting by SilverWood Books

SUZANNE STEWART writes song lyrics, poems and short plays which have been performed at local festivals in the Bristol area. She is generally interested in music, and has been a drummer, which tends to creep into her stories! She also writes articles about cats, family life and school stories; they have been published in various magazines under the name of Sue Weekes.

Sue belongs to a writing group, Café Corner Writers, which has produced anthologies they also use for performances – the most recent one is *Beauty and The Beast*. She's also coordinated a songwriting collective, Act of Faith, and worked on literacy projects in schools and adult educational centres.

Since leaving her full-time job as a careers adviser, Sue has had more time to concentrate on her writing, and has now completed a young adult novel set in the Bronze Age, but with a modern twist – *Rowan The Dreamweaver*. This is meant to be the first in a trilogy, and she has already started working on Book 2.

You can find out more about Sue's writing through her Facebook page: facebook.com/rowanthedreamweaver

Rowan the Dreamweaver

THANKS

To my chapter-by-chapter first readers Emma, Gill and Jane.
You joined Rowan on her journey!

To Sarah for proofreading.

To Carole, Nic and Sharon for general support.

To Paige for artwork that helped with the cover.

To Melissa for being a fellow writer in the family.

To Amz in the hope H. will like it too.

To Tony for writing inspiration.

And especially to Missy, my typing companion and the inspiration behind Kezzie.

PLACE NAMES

The Big River = the Severn

The Green Isle = Ireland

The Henge = temple at Avebury
(but if you want to think of it as Stonehenge, that's fine)

The Middle Sea = the Mediterranean

The Shallow Sea = the Channel

INTRO

"So the harpist was the rock god of the Bronze Age," their teacher tells the class wandering round the museum. "Singer, songwriter and stringed instrument player."

"This harp looks pretty small," says one girl. "I always thought they were whacking great things."

"Sounds OK, whatever," her friend says, "and look at this other stuff they played. If we could go back in a time machine, we could meet some hot boys with bands!"

"The harp players didn't always have an easy life," the teacher says. "They didn't just entertain the troops, they were expected to go into battle with them!"

"What about the women?" another female member of the class asks.

"Oh, they seem to have been pretty economically active. Weavers, herbalists, artists, priestesses and so on, as well as homemakers and bakers. You can see two head-and-shoulder pictures of two young women from about the middle Bronze Age on these large pebbles here."

"I think it's great they were preserved so long," one of the boys says. "The dark-haired one still looks really cute."

"You reckon? I like the other one," his friend says.

"Well, if you go for ginger mi—um, skinny girls with red hair and freckles…"

For a moment, the friend's head looks as if it's being pulled down towards the case. Then he straightens up and rubs his eyes.

"I like this one," he says. "She's got an interesting face."

CHAPTER 1

"It's not fair! It's not fair! It's not fair!"

I'm screaming this into my shell and thumping my bedding (which is tough – I wove it myself!) when I feel Kezzie land on my back and walk up my spine.

"Falling out with your mother?" she purrs.

That's a pretty easy guess. Of course, to my mother it would just sound like Kezzie purring. But Kezzie and I have understood each other ever since she was a kitten and my foster aunt Jelize (when she gave up being a priestess) brought her back from the Great Henge for me.

"It's really serious this time," I say, twisting myself round so I can look into Kezzie's amber eyes as she slides to my side. "She's trying to stop me going to the big autumn festival. All us two-legs know, when you've turned fourteen years old, you count as a full member of the tribe and you're meant to attend. Besides, I really, really want to go. And for you to come too."

"Does your mother dislike these festivals because your father was killed building one of your stone temples?"

(You can't say I get all this in exact human speech from Kezzie. But I get it from pictures in her head, or just a kind of sympathetic feeling.)

"I don't think it's that. It's not as if the festival's at the same henge, even. And she could let me go with cousin Anyanda's family – they'll be off selling their beakers as usual."

"And you'd like to do that?"

"No, I want to sell my own work. And I am fourteen, even if Great-Uncle Ig tried to make out I was thirteen and there must have been a slip cutting the age notches on my reckoning stick – thinking he was helping my mother. He knows" —I peer down at the still newish dark blue tattoo snaking its way up my left forearm— "I'd not have been made a Dragon otherwise. So I'm old enough to be allowed my own stall and to sell my own weaving."

"Shame for you two-legs you don't have beautiful natural fur," Kezzie tells me as she starts grooming herself. "But it's a good thing for you that you can create it for them. And at least your way – getting wool sheared from sheep and colouring it – doesn't harm any living creatures."

"Well, I know I'm a good weaver, even if my mother thinks some of my designs are too fancy. But I want to see how I'll get on selling clothes and cloths I've made to folk from all over the country – other parts of the world, even."

Kezzie purrs reassuringly.

"So it's because of your work you want to go? Have you explained that to your mother? Tell her I'll protect you!"

I hug my knees.

"It's everything! It's wanting to get away from a little village where I've lived for ever, and letting my whole grown-up life begin."

"Rowan."

It's my mother in the doorway. I look at her defiantly, and Kezzie looks rather scornful. She reckons my mother could talk to her directly if her mind wasn't closed to it.

"I suppose you're sulking about the festival."

I want to argue about the word 'sulking'. But my mother is quite an imposing figure when she towers over you. She's taller than most people hereabouts, and paler. And as she's a herbalist, she knows how to keep her hair jet-black, even though she's pushing thirty. When her grey eyes glitter at you in a frosty sort of way, she looks like a spirit of winter.

"Well," I say as politely as possible, "I think I have a justifiable grievance."

"Why," my mother asks, sitting heavily on the end of my sleeping couch, "is it so important to you?"

"Well, because of my trade… Oh, and the spiritual side, of course. Services in the temple, um, singing the earth into her winter sleep – all that."

My mother, who isn't a very religious woman, sniffs rather scornfully. "So it's not about meeting young men?"

I'm genuinely horrified. "Of course not! I'm not like Anyanda!"

"Well, no," my mother agrees, smiling faintly. "But it is quite customary for young men to ride off with young women at the end of the week – or, at least, to expect they'll jump the bonfire together."

"Yes, but nowadays they only ride off with a girl who's given her consent first, honestly." (My mother hasn't gone to a big henge festival since I've known her, so you can't expect her to be up to date.) "And usually the families have agreed. Anyanda's told me all about it."

"I hope they do. But that's not the point. I don't want you to do anything so foolish as to marry someone whom you've only known for a few days on a holiday occasion."

"Like she did," Kezzie murmurs in my ear. My mother looks at her suspiciously, but it makes sense to me. Although my mother never talks about her childhood, she doesn't come from the west – even her accent's a bit sharper. She plainly didn't want to return to her original tribe after my father's death, since she stayed here and moved my father's old uncle in, so she'd got a man about the house; as he's a bit wandering in his wits, it's really us looking after him, but he is helpful with odd jobs like sweeping and washing.

"Anyway," my mother continues in a resigned sort of way, "I've decided you'd better go. But only on condition I come with you, so I can keep an eye on you. And when we're there, I want you to have nothing to do with any Hawks you might come across."

I can go! That's all I care about.

"Of course I don't mind if you come, though Kezzie will look after me. I don't want to talk to hawks either – I mean, it's only Kezzie I can talk to, and she's a lynx – I don't talk to birds."

My mother sighs. "I mean members of the Hawk tribe."

"Oh, our so-called tribal overlords. That rich, powerful lot from up north. I bet they're all swollen-headed, and I won't want to talk to them anyway," I agree hastily. "But may I go and scry Anyanda, to tell her I can come?"

"She only lives three hundred paces away! But yes, scry her if you must."

I've prepared my basin of steaming water, scooped from our ever-boiling cauldron, with pinches of helpful herbs, and call to my cousin in my head. Anyanda's not the easiest person to contact by scrying – even when you're in the same room or field, she doesn't always listen to you properly. She's a bit opaque like that, and so is Aunt Anya, her mother. But this time she responds at once, and I see a laughing face framed in dark curls appear beneath the bubbles.

"My mother says I can go!"

"That's wonderful! I've arranged to see Jelize tomorrow to get my love token painted – you'll have to come with me. Can you be at my home three hours after sun-up?"

"I think so," I say cautiously. Being a weaver does make me a bit more flexible about when I work, especially when nights are still light. I don't know about love tokens; they don't sound like something my mother would approve of – I vaguely know they're pebbles with your portrait which you can give to a boy if you actually want him to run off with you – but if Jelize is doing the painting, that should be all right.

"So you are going to the Great Henge?" someone murmurs behind me. Of course it's Uncle Ig, who has a habit of slipping up quietly behind you, despite being creaky with the arthritis all my mother's nettle poultices can never totally cure. "I never thought your mother would agree. It's very brave of Raven after what happened."

"My father was doing restoration work on a henge and was killed by an accidental fall soon after I was born," I say impatiently. "You can't expect me never to go anywhere on that account! Or my mother, either."

"Accidental?" Uncle Ig sounds surprised. Then he blinks his watery eyes at me. "Oh, yes. I'd forgotten she told me to tell you that."

Come this new morning, I'm still trying to shrug off my uncle's unsettling remark… It's a crisp blue leaf-fall day, and going to seeing Jelize at her hut in the clearing, where she tends her crops and chickens (for their eggs – she doesn't eat meat) always makes me happy. She's a bit younger than my mother, and she's someone I've always been able to talk to about things that matter to me. Ever since she came back to the village, she's run a little school in return for other goods, like crockery from my cousin's family, who were the ones who brought her up from when she was a foundling baby – left at the Great Henge, funnily enough. Most children, and their parents, just want her to teach basic numbering, memorising and drawing symbols, but she taught me a lot more – which, to be fair, my mother was fine with; she thinks women should know everything from carpentry to astronomy, without depending on a man. I've even learned a bit of Egyptian from Jelize, which she learned when she was a priestess – now there's a country I'd love to travel to. Sometimes I dream I'm flying over one of their towns with tall white buildings, dazzling beneath a burning-bright sky.

"And I'll be coming to the festival with you," Jelize tells me, as I sit in the sunlight while she works on Anyanda's stone.

Her hair looks like gold in the sun; most of us are dark, and despite my red hair even I've got the same dark eyes as my father's forebears – the ones who came across the Shallow Sea selling beakers generations ago.

"Oh, that's wonderful! Is that because my mother and I are going? And Kezzie, of course," I add as Kezzie growls.

"Well, I'll enjoy travelling with you, and the rest of the family. But I was asked to be there."

Anyanda and I exchange wary glances. It's rare for someone to leave the priesthood on the sort of terms that mean they can go back. But Jelize, who is usually so happy to talk about anything from beekeeping to birthing children, will never talk about her life in the temple. (I know she totally disagreed with animal sacrifices, but there must be more to it.)

"That should dry nicely before I seal it," Jelize continues as she puts down Anyanda's token. "Your turn, Rowan."

Suddenly I feel oddly alarmed. "I'm not sure…"

Jelize looks amused. "You don't have to give it to a young man if no one takes your fancy by the end of the week. Put it in a box, throw it in a bog – maybe it'll surface in a few thousand years' time!"

CHAPTER 2

"So," says Beaver Boy, "what competitions are you thinking of entering? Double fish," he adds.

That last bit refers to a game he's teaching Anyanda, which involves fish bones – what else would you expect from a member of the Beaver tribe? – and a lot of giggling on her part. He's even got broad white teeth which gleam in the light from our campfire. It's handy, though, that our two parties fell in with each other, as theirs headed up from the marshy coastal lands to the south.

"I expect Rowan will go in for the weaving," Anyanda says.

"And you? You look like a girl with a lot of talents."

Anyanda smirks. "Oh, I have. But I'm more of a businesswoman, even if my father's an artist – with beaker designs, you know. So I'll be helping Rowan on her stall."

"Very helpful, too," Beaver Boy approves.

I have to suppress a smile. I'm not saying my cousin doesn't genuinely want to use her trading talents on my behalf. But I also reckon she wants the chance to flirt with young men out of her mother's sight. I know that my aunt's keen that her youngest child, and only surviving daughter, makes what she'll consider a good marriage. And Anyanda doesn't seem to mind this like I would. Only – being a girl who thinks bronze was invented to provide her with mirrors – she wants to have some fun first.

"Well, my brother came second in the archery contest last time we were here," his sister chips in. (She's a haughty-looking person, about twenty – a bit old to be unwed, unless of course you're a priestess, but apparently she's going to marry some village elder back home.) "The person who came first should have turned twenty-one by now, so he won't be eligible for the same matches. So my brother will be a sure-fire winner."

"Awww, sis…" Beaver Boy bats away her remark with a wave of his hand, but you can tell he agrees. No one had told me there were going to be competitions! Here we are, only another day's journey away from the Great Henge. This keeps getting better. Except…

"I suppose you can go in for more than one challenge?" I ask. "I wouldn't mind trying archery too. Not," I add for politeness's sake, "that I'll be as good as you. But my cousin can tell you I usually do best out of anyone in our village when we have our Sun's Day afternoon practices."

"Well, you won't be allowed to apply," his sister says, sounding pleased about it. "No females are allowed to enter for archery or swordplay."

"But that's so wrong!" I start to stand up, and Kezzie pulls me back by my skirt. I carry on in a milder way. "After all, we all practise archery at home."

"You Dragons may," Beaver Boy explains in a more kindly way. "But not all tribes do. Not Beavers to start with. Nor Hawks."

I feel less impressed than ever by what I've heard of the Hawks.

"And those the priests and priestesses appoint to organise these events must draw a line somewhere," the sister says smugly. "You'll be expecting them to allow women harpists next. Or do you have them back in Dragon-Land?"

"No, we just have travelling men," I admit. "But if there are women harpists out there, I don't see why—"

"Ssh," Beaver Boy says, and we all listen intently to what sounds like wolves howling in the distance. Kezzie stiffens beside me.

"It's really good we all met up to be company for each other," I say in a voice which is meant to be light-hearted but comes out a bit squeaky. "Great fish stews, thanks to you!"

Beaver Boy looks at me curiously. "You worried about wolves? I reckoned you for a wild-animal charmer. After all, you've got a pet lynx!"

Kezzie growls, but in rather an amused way.

"She's my friend," I explain. "We grew up together after Jelize stopped being a priestess and brought Kezzie home with her."

"Your Jelize is a funny one," Beaver Boy says, looking at where Jelize sits on my rugs a little apart from the rest of us, her face turned up to the starlight as she meditates. "Is she your aunt?"

"Well, sort of. She's my uncle's foster sister."

"That's my father. The head of our village," Anyanda says pointedly.

Beaver Boy's sister glances dismissively at Uncle Bram, who is talking, laughing and drinking mead with other men from both tribes by a larger campfire.

"But you, Rowan Ravensdaughter. You live only with your mother?"

"And Great-Uncle Ig. He lodges with us."

"So your mother has no husband."

"No. She doesn't want another one."

Both Beavers seem to find this strange. But the brother looks a bit sorry for me, whereas his sister just sniffs disdainfully.

"That's the wolves again," Anyanda says. "They sound closer." Then, turning to Beaver Boy, "You will protect me, won't you?"

"They sound more like human wolves," he replies, his hand going to his dagger as if by instinct.

"Are they from another tribe?" I ask.

"Not really," he explains curtly. "Unless you count those who've banded together because they're fugitives from justice."

As Kezzie snuggles against me, giving me reassuring licks, Uncle Bram leaves the group of men and strides towards us.

"All right, young 'uns, we need to form a circle around the fire. Daughter – help those tending to the horses. Rowan – you've brought your bow and arrows – say a prayer to the Goddess and get ready to shoot."

I nod a reply to my uncle, feeling my throat tighten a little. I've enjoyed archery as a sport for so long that I've almost forgotten its original purpose as a weapon of war. Bram arranges us in two circles, the fires both behind and before us. I notice that although Bram confers with the older men among the Beavers, they seem happy to let him take overall charge. I can't help feeling a bit proud of my uncle.

"And I gather you two are our young champions," he says to me and Beaver Boy. "So you'd best be on the outside."

Beaver Boy and I exchange small smiles. A flame leaps up and shows the nervousness in his eyes (dark like mine and Anyanda's). Oddly, this heartens me. As we take our positions, the human wolf howls – which have been coming closer – fall suddenly silent. I wonder for one wild moment if that means the outlaws have gone away.

"They're nearly upon us," Bram says quietly.

Then, to the surprise of us all, Jelize steps forward, carrying a brand of wood as torchlight. "Let me try another way first," she says to Bram.

After a moment's pause he nods, and she walks off in the direction where the wolf howls were loudest. I can hardly believe this is happening.

"I must follow her," I mutter to Beaver Boy, and slip away into the darkness of a clouded night. I hear Bram call "Rowan", but he doesn't call very loudly. I stop my ears and focus on the flame ahead.

Jelize arrives at a patch of open ground, and sticks her torch in the damp earth.

"People of the Wolf," she calls. "What do you want from us?"

I hope they understand her, but most folk in our country speak some kind of British tongue, though I gather it changes a lot in the north. Anyway, this lot must follow her, because a man steps into the clearing. He doesn't look too thin, or badly dressed, but maybe he's one of their leaders.

"What do you think?" he asks curtly. "Food, and maybe other supplies you carry."

"And if we agree to leave some here for you, will you leave our camp in peace?"

"What kind of travellers are you? Are there no warriors among you?"

"Oh, we have a good fighting force," Jelize says coolly. "But we also have a little spare dried meat and fish, vegetables and woven wool. If by giving them to you we save bloodshed on our way to a holy festival, surely we all win?"

The moon slides out, and I see the man pulling at his straggly beard. His hand is missing a couple of fingers.

"Well, I've no wish to offend those under the protection of the Goddess. I tell you what – if you can throw in a couple of cooking pots, since ours are getting worn, it's a bargain!"

Jelize inclines her head. "Then leave, and when we

can tell by the faint wolf howls that you are truly at some distance, we will return to this clearing with the goods as promised. But we will come armed, so no treachery!" Jelize appears to grow a bit taller as she says this, and I can see a kind of lightning flicker around her. I think the outlaw chief can too, because he backs away hastily.

"None – I swear by the Goddess."

After a pause while he moves away, Jelize turns. "It's all right, Rowan," she says softly, "you can come out from behind your tree now."

And Kezzie comes bounding out from behind me – I hadn't realised she was there. Quite a family party!

At first I'm a bit sulky – I'd thought my woodcraft was better than that – but I'm also curious. "That wolf-man – he really seemed to respect religion. And he could see things like – well, like I can."

"Oh, Rowan," Jelize laughs gently, "it's not just the respectable and law-abiding who have rights to that kind of awareness. And we don't know what misfortune rather than wrongdoing may have brought him to this..."

"What about other travellers, though? Aren't we just making the wolf-men stronger to attack them?"

"Yes," Jelize says sadly, "but we can hope we've helped them learn there are other paths to go down."

"Well, I'm not sorry we're not fighting," I admit. "I was pretty scared."

"But you were the one who came after me, Rowan. I won't forget that. By the way, I hope you won't mind giving up a couple of the plain tunics in your stock?"

"Not for a reason like this. But I don't think Aunt Anya will be happy about the cooking pots – after all, she's the only one who's brought extra favourites with her!"

*

And I'm proved right.

"You selfish woman, Jelize Nomanschild," my aunt rants. "You don't know how much these pots cost in fine drinking vessels!"

"Well, no. But don't you think they're a worthy price for saving a number of lives?"

"Jelize is right, my dear," Bram says. "And as village heads we must be prepared to set a good example by making some small sacrifices."

I wonder if she agrees. When we forded the river on our way here, Aunt Anya threw in some hairpins to make sure the water spirits keep it low for us on our return. My mother sniffed, and said that will simply depend on how soon the winter rains come, and she agrees with the weather-tellers it should stay fine until after the autumn solstice – good news for the festival! Jelize, who can see nature spirits, said she wasn't sure what they'd want with hairpins. To which Aunt Anya replied it was the thought that counted; and my mother pointed out that only throwing in old bent pins you no longer use isn't much of a thought, either.

I also wonder for a moment if my uncle wouldn't be happier with someone like Jelize, who shares more of his outlook on life. But it's Aunt Anya – who, we all know, still runs the clay and beaker works their sons and daughters-in-law are meant to be in charge of – who really makes their business a success, however good my uncle is at designs.

Beaver Boy is another one who isn't too happy about our change in plans. "We could have fought," he protests, coming up to Bram and Jelize. "I wasn't afraid."

"Of course not," Jelize says swiftly. "But at least you can show us your skills at the archery contest."

"Yes." Beaver Boy cheers up, and turns to Anyanda. "And I will present you with the first prize."

"If you win it – and I decide to accept it." Anyanda sounds a bit sharp.

"Well, time to sleep, youngsters," Bram says hastily. "Now the days draw short, we need to breakfast by sunrise."

"Rowan," Anyanda says softly, as we snuggle beneath our blankets, Kezzie between us, "I think you should go in for that archery contest."

"Me? But you heard that Beaver girl say I can't – and I'm already going in for weaving."

My cousin sits up, hugging her knees.

"Oh Rowan, have a bit of initiative," she scoffs. "Stick your hair under a cap and call yourself 'Mab from the Mountains'. No one will know."

"It sounds worth a try," I say cautiously, "but what happens if I get found out?"

"Oh, nothing," Anyanda says airily – too much so for my liking. "It's not as if it's anything to do with the religious part of the festival."

"Well, why are you so keen for me to do it?"

My cousin pauses before answering.

"Because I want a certain young man to realise he's not the only one who can aim true and hit a mark."

"You do?" I lean up on one elbow. "But I thought you quite liked him. Even if he is a bit of a bighead – and not specially good-looking—"

"What are you talking about?" Anyanda snaps. "He's extremely handsome."

Kezzie licks my hand. I can hear her telling me, "Your cousin really likes this boy."

"Oh well. I know I'm no judge," I mollify Anyanda.

"No," she agrees, "and you will compete?"

"It sounds like the sort of thing you two-legs find fun," Kezzie purrs.

"All right," I say. "But it better not lead to any trouble if I'm caught!"

CHAPTER 3

"…So I said to him, 'You can brag all you like about your pyramids, but I'll bet they're not a patch on our henges!'"

"Well, having seen both, I'd say they're both striking in different ways. But when I was in the Greek Isles…"

This is marvellous! I can't help hugging myself in delight as I hear people go past the stall, talking with strange accents of faraway places. A number of them stop at the stall, too. I think my display's pretty eye-catching, but I'm glad of Anyanda, who knows what she's doing when it comes to trade.

"You've got to be careful with someone who wants to barter," she explains. "Take proper metals, or small objects you can sell or trade with back home. No livestock, unless your group really needs it. No shells – some folk from the north-east use them as tokens among themselves, but they're no good anywhere else. Unless it's a really good one that you could turn into a speaking shell, or ornament, be firm and refuse them!"

Mind you, I did feel a bit unsure last night about having come to trade. We all went to one of the Sun's Day evening services to give thanks for our safe arrival, pray for guidance in the coming week, and think of the spirits of our dead, who, some folk say, draw especially close at this time of year. The processions and chanting as the sun went down made the hairs rise on the back of my neck (like Kezzie's might have, although she wouldn't go into the temple). Then us younger women were taken to a side chapel for a talk from some junior priestess – stuff we all know, like the three aspects of the Goddess being virgin hunter, mother and harvester, and wise old crone with healing powers. But I was struck by her point about us being here for reflection, not just trade and feasting. I even said afterwards maybe I should take time to attend more services. But Anyanda pointed out we'd already got a space booked for our stall, while my mother sniffed and said she thought the strong incense had gone to my head. And today – today I'm very glad I took their advice (for once).

"Yes, I think the dark green cloak with the red-leaf border would suit my son. This is very finely woven."

A pretty, dark-haired woman, dressed quite finely herself, is fingering the choices.

"Nothing but the finest wool and best dyes," Anyanda assures her.

"Also, I especially like the pattern," the woman explains, in an accent I can't quite place – soft, but with a northern overlay. "It's very original."

"Oh, that's my cousin here – Rowan the Weaver. She makes up designs out of her own head."

"Really? Then I must send my son to you. And his friends. They're musicians, you see. They like to stand out from the crowd. Maybe matching tunics for their performances…"

"So they're here, at the festival?" my cousin asks eagerly.

"Oh yes," the woman says vaguely, as she beckons a servant to come and take the cloak while she pays in jewellery without any quibble. "If they do turn up, my son's Kelvan, the harpist."

She drifts off, and Anyanda grabs my arm with excitement. "Oh, Rowan! That proves you were right – to weave according to your own imagination, whatever your mother said."

"Well," I say, rubbing my arm, "she seemed a nice lady, and Kezzie liked her. But she's not the first person today who's praised my designs. In case you'd not noticed."

"No, but she's Kelvan's mother! That means all the musicians here may be coming to us!"

I don't know what's so exciting about that. And if my cousin's looking forward to meeting more young men, maybe I should remind her about Beaver Boy, whom we've not seen yet today – probably off in some field practising his archery.

"I've heard," I say cautiously, "that musicians aren't always the best payers."

"No, but they set the fashion for all the young people here," Anyanda says impatiently. "And you don't need to worry about this lot – if they don't pay, their parents will. You'll be made for life if you get taken under the wing of the Hawks!"

I think about this as the sun reaches its maximum height and trade slows down. No doubt everyone's eating, answering calls of nature and so on – as we three do in turn. I wonder how serious my mother was when she told me to stay away from the Hawk tribe. Unfortunately, she doesn't tend to say anything she's not serious about!

As Kezzie, Anyanda and I all settle behind our stall again, I see a group of young men staggering up Cloth Alley, as it's known for now. We're forbidden to drink alcohol until the evening feasts in the halls, but I guess this lot have got hold of mead from somewhere – one's still carrying a flask and raising it to his lips. They come to a stop in front of our stall. I notice each of them is wearing a wool plait pinned to his real hair – which seems to be a fashion this festival among the younger folk. I reckon I could get Anyanda to help me run up a few for our stall.

"Some nice outfits, lads," one of them says, "and something even nicer behind them."

Another one leers at us, only it comes out cross-eyed. "How much for a trip to the woods with you two?"

"And what would you pay us with?" my cousin asks sharply. "Shells?"

I've been thinking these might be the Hawks we were told to expect – and if so, my mother was quite right about them! But it sounds as if Anyanda knows them for members of the tribe from the north-east.

"Don't tell me you wouldn't enjoy it yourself. You look the type, even if lynx girl here" —the speaker glances at me and Kezzie— "doesn't." He lurches towards my cousin. Kezzie growls loudly and he falls against the counter, then slides down in front of it. "By the Goddess's tits!" he swears.

I'm a bit shocked by this blasphemy so near holy ground. (Yes, I know Jelize would say all ground is holy.) But I also can't help laughing as the young man gazes around him, wondering how he comes to be sitting on the hard-trodden dried earth. His friends don't like this, and move in menacingly.

"Do you want any help, young ladies?"

I hear the voice before I see the older person who parts the shell-traders. I realise it's a thick-set, sun-tanned man I've seen before – he's the one with a foreign accent who went past talking to someone else who was trying to convince him henges are better built than pyramids. I can also see two other men – maybe servants, but certainly big and muscly – standing behind them, plus three more trying to blend in with the now-thickening crowd, but looking as though they're on the alert for trouble. The Shell folk don't like the look of them, and start backing off.

Anyanda smiles up at him. He's older than her father, to judge by his greying hair and beard, but she still puts on this flirtatious manner. "Just a bit of trouble with these impertinent louts, sir."

The man frowns. "You girls seem rather young – and pretty – to be trading alone. Have you no family? No elders from your tribe to hand?"

"My mother's selling herbs just at the top of the lane round the corner," I explain.

The man nods to the two servants (bodyguards?). "I'll take this young lady to her mother, to explain what's happened. You can stay here until I return."

"We are grown women," I protest, "and traders in our own right. We don't need—"

Kezzie's bounding round from the side of the stall, and I think she may chase this person away. But he stands his ground, and she leaps up and licks him. He bends down to stroke her head, and she rubs against his hand.

"All right then," I say ungraciously. "I'll come."

"I suppose we should introduce ourselves. I'm Ezra."

The crowd's thickening up, but he seems good at marching on, so it parts before him.

"Oh," I say politely, "I'm Rowan Ravensdaughter. You're...?"

"Ah. Ezra ben Simeon. Ezra son of Simeon. But just Ezra will do fine."

"So Simeon was your mother?"

"No – my father. And still is, I trust. I've not been back home for three years, but I intend to head that way after this trip. I'd forgotten you all take your mother's name here."

"Well, it makes sense, doesn't it? You know for sure who a child's mother is. Well, usually," I add, thinking of Jelize.

"And is your father at this festival?"

"No." I'm getting a bit tired of questions – though Kezzie still seems happy enough as she leaps along. "My mother's a widow. And herbalist. My father restored henges."

"Both worthy callings... No doubt your temples need work doing on them – this one's plainly been here for some long time. Good site for it, too. Between hills and river."

"Well, it was a sacred site before we built here," I explain. "One of the thin places."

"Thin?" Ezra sounds puzzled.

"Well – you know how there's normally a kind of curtain between our world and that of Spirit?"

Ezra agrees, to my relief – I don't know how I'd have gone on explaining otherwise.

"And there are some places where it's more like a thin veil," I go on more confidently. "This is one of them."

"And how in Yahweh's – God's – name did your people move these huge stones to this site?"

"Well, some of them were lying around anyway, I think. The rest we specially transported from the west of Britain. It was done by – oh, that's my mother," I say, with some relief, saved from giving a history lesson, as we round the corner.

My mother stands on a rise at the top of the lane, arms folded and gazing haughtily about her.

(I guess that although she does well enough at home, where she's known, she's not much of a saleswoman, and maybe that's another reason why she's not keen on festivals. Anyanda could do the patter for her – "Oh, yes, I picked this agrimony by full moon, to enhance its powers." But my mother doesn't say charms over her wares. Not that I agree with her; I reckon thoughts count – like bread rising better if you bake with a light heart.)

Ezra has seemed dumbstruck. But as I look at him, he asks, "That magnificent woman's your mother?"

"Well, that's my mother, Raven, all right," I say edging a little away from him.

Ezra's seemed quite normal until now, but people can get a bit strange with age, and I'm sure he's pushing forty.

"That hair!" he exclaims, still gazing. "It's fine up – she looks like a queen in Egypt. Unbound it must be a wonderful sight."

Oh, for the Goddess's sake! I see my mother's hair down every evening. And while I admit she knows what washes to steep it in so it stays black and shiny, it's still just hair!

"So after this Ezra man has been so kind as to protect our girls from the east coast barbarians, I thought the least I could do was to ask him to join us in our dining hall," my mother explains to Jelize, Aunt Anya and Anyanda as we all change for the evening meal. "A lone traveller, far from home…"

Yes, poor lonely Ezra with his fleet of servant bodyguards (one of whom he's offering to watch over me and Anyanda for the following days of the festival).

"So what does he trade in?" Jelize asks.

"Precious stones – and metals – and ready-made jewellery."

All our eyes are drawn at once to the gems sparkling around her neck.

"Did he give you that necklace?" Aunt Anya asks.

(If he did, I've missed seeing it. But they did talk while my mother sent me to fetch her some fresh bread. Sometimes my aunt's bluntness can be useful.)

"Just a trinket he happened to have with him, which I'm now wearing as a mark of politeness." But my mother hums as she combs her hair, and I get a picture of a stream flowing merrily under ice before the spring thaw.

"He must carry expensive trinkets," Aunt Anya sniffs. "I suppose he's based up near the Hawks' camp – they're the sort of tribe a man like him would trade with."

"Well," Anyanda breaks in excitedly, "we made a good sale to a Hawk lady today. And she's Kelvan's mother, and she's going to send him and his band of musicians to us."

"Kelvan?" Aunt Anya asks in a puzzled tone.

"Kelvan Windhawk's a harpist," Jelize explains. "Very highly thought of, at least by other young people."

(My aunt and mother don't know much about modern music.)

My mother suddenly freezes again, though I feel fire under ice. She throws down her comb and swings round to face me. "Rowan, what did I tell you about the Hawks?"

"To have nothing to do with them. But music's not about tribes, it's for everyone. The same as weaving, really."

"And," Anyanda adds, "what have you got against the Hawks, Aunt Raven? After all, you're one of them."

Well. To think I hadn't realised. Her name – and even mine – should have given it away. But why such a mystery? Is this to do with my father, too?

My mother looks cross with Anyanda, and I'm feeling pretty angry myself. But just as we're all staring and glaring at each other, and Kezzie's slunk into a corner with hackles raised, we hear Uncle Bram outside our shelter.

"Excuse me, ladies. May I come in?"

"Oh, very well." But my aunt sounds even more impatient with her husband than usual. Of course, he doesn't know what he's interrupting.

He enters in his usual, rather mild way, as if checking we're all decently clothed first. Then he stands up, though still stooped under our low roof, and says in a rather bewildered voice, "There's a young man outside. Asking where he can find Rowan."

Now we all look surprised. We expect young men to ask for Anyanda.

"Is it our Beaver friend?" Anyanda can't stop herself asking eagerly. "He might have got our names mixed up."

"No," her father says, tugging on his beard. "This is someone called Kelvan Windhawk. He's got some friends with him. And a harp."

And I can see that for myself as soon as I get outside. One young man a bit to the foreground, three more lurking behind him. They look a bit older than me – maybe fifteen, like Anyanda, or even sixteen. The first one, the one with the harp slung round him, comes up and says, in quite a polite and pleasant sort of voice, "Are you Rowan the Weaver? My mother advised me to come and see you."

As he says this, several things pass through my mind.

- It's nice to be addressed as 'Rowan the Weaver' not 'Rowan Ravensdaughter'.

- The harpist is what I'd call rather good-looking. His hair's dark brown, like his mother's, but spiky and ruffled by the breeze; and he's got the same sea-blue eyes, and he looks pretty muscular. Thinnish, but definitely muscular. Quite tall and bony – typical Hawk – and a springy sort of walk, as if he's not quite touching the ground.

- I'm glad I'm wearing my feasting dress – saffron, embroidered with imported brown silk thread – at least I can design colours that suit me!

But at the back of my mind, there's a picture of a large shell, two halves fanned open, but now they're moving together.

The harpist gives me a puzzled glance. I'm used to thinking several things at once while men finish a sentence, but in this case I may have been a bit slow. Anyanda, who has bustled out behind me, gives me a poke in the back.

"This is my cousin, Rowan," she explains. "She's a bit quiet" —Thanks!— "but she's an excellent weaver. As you can see. We're both wearing her creations."

This is true. Anyanda's gown is dark red with silver thread. I'm not sure, judging by her simper as she says this, how much she's concerned about my work and how much she doesn't want to leave handsome harpists to me, whatever she feels for Beaver Boy.

His glance flicks over her gown – not the person inside, despite the tight fitting she insisted on for her bodice. "Yes, I can see that's great workmanship," he agrees. Then he bends down to Kezzie, who has also followed me. "Aren't you a beauty?" he says, kneeling so she can lick his hands and face. "Are you a friend of the family?"

"She's my best friend, and she's called Kezzie," I explain approvingly.

"And I'm Anyanda. My father's the chief of our village." She sounds a bit sour, but keen to salvage the social situation.

"Oh yes." The harpist straightens up. "I'm Kelvan Windhawk, or Kelvan the Harpist. These" —with a wave to his friends, who draw closer— "are Mart – short for Pine Marten – Sparrowhawk, or Sparrow, and Crow. This is Sparrow's dog, Snapper."

A small dog, obviously more pet than hunting or guard dog, comes out from behind Sparrow. Snapper and Kezzie sniff at each other warily, then decide to make friends.

"Don't forget your 'Prince' part," the stocky, dark one – Mart – interrupts rather drily.

Kelvan shrugs. "I don't use the title."

"But you are a prince, really?" asks Anyanda.

Mart laughs, a bit scornfully. "His grandfather's only King of the Northlands. No doubt your overlord. His mother's father's a king in the Green Isle."

"But only a small one, not the High King. They go in for grand names, my mother's people. It's not much different to being head of a village over here."

"Not exactly—" Mart seems inclined to argue, but Kelvan throws him a quelling glance.

"As I was saying, Mart plays the horn. Sometimes we let him have solos. Sparrow plays strings" —of course, some people do, adapting bow and arrow— "and bones – he's pretty versatile really. Crow" —he gestures towards a tall, gangling young man, with an amiable, toothy grin— "Crow's the drummer – well, someone has to be!"

"In some countries," Crow says to me and Anyanda – mostly looking at her – "drummers are given great respect. According to travellers' tales, in both cold countries to the north and hot ones to the south, no religious ceremony can be held without them."

"Maybe these other countries haven't developed such a range of instruments as we have," Kelvan suggests.

"Or maybe," Mart adds, under his breath but so we can all hear him, "they've developed a better class of drummer!"

The musicians all laugh, even Crow. Why are young men so mean to each other? The boys back home are the same. I still feel impelled to add, in a bright voice, "In Egypt they've got a great variety of musical instruments. And women play the harp!"

Three of the men stare at me, and I realise music must be like beers and spears back home: topics where women aren't expected to have an opinion. My mother and Jelize sometimes laugh about it. But Kelvan just asks in an ordinary way, "Have you ever been to Egypt, Rowan?"

I don't know how he thinks I'd have had the chance – but it's better than his friends looking as if I've grown a spare head.

"No, but I've met a man from a land near there, who knows Egypt well."

"Oh, Ezra ben Simeon! My mother's delighted he's here again. My father will be pleased for her – he suggested she came with me to have a short break from managing our household, and see if she can pick up some jewels to her taste. Of course, our band's hoping to move on to other settlements – maybe other festivals. Our families have agreed we can have a year to do this, before returning to the trades we're meant to follow."

"Well, that will be good in itself," Sparrow points out. He and Mart look quite pleased at the thought of their future careers, whatever they may be, while Kelvan looks a bit gloomy, and Crow just vague. "And we've got a pact with each other – no bonfire-jumping till the year's up!"

Rich people are certainly different. But this reminds me what we're meant to be talking about.

"Your mother thought you might have a commission for me," I remind him.

"Tunics," Kelvan explains. "The same colour, so we'll look good playing together. Have you any in stock?"

"Well, yes. Plain, or saffron. The second would be more striking, if they'll fit you all – at least, wool can stretch. Of course, I've no time to weave new ones, but I could embroider an emblem on each in black, ready for this time tomorrow. If you don't mind paying extra."

Kelvan snaps his fingers. "Excellent! My mother was right to recommend you." He turns to his friends. "What design shall we have, lads?"

Mart replies. (Sparrow seems shy, and Crow just keeps staring at my cousin.) "Suppose we'd better have hawks. What else?"

"Yes, what else?" Kelvan agrees, with a bit of a sigh.

"They'll look really striking," I say enthusiastically.

Kelvan appears to cheer up. "Yes, they'll look good."

"And Prince – uh, Kelvan Windhawk," Anyanda butts

in. "I know this'll get my cousin's work noticed, but what about the payment?"

"Oh yes," Kelvan says vaguely, "I'll get my mother to see to all that. Will you be dining in the westward banqueting hall tonight?"

"I think so. Won't all the Dragons be there?" I ask.

Kelvan grins. "Well," he says, "then we might see you later."

CHAPTER 4

"So," Ezra smiles, "this is an excellent feast. Better than when I was here five years ago."

"You've remembered how to speak British very well," I say, both politely and truthfully.

"It's useful to know the languages of those I do most trade with. I usually hire a local lad as one of my staff – if he seems trustworthy – so we can talk on the road."

"You don't seem to trust our mead or beer, though," I say as I see Ezra pour a darker, thinner liquid from a small flask into his cup. "Do you think you'll be poisoned?"

Ezra laughs. "I never trust foreign drink. You can't tell what effect it might have on you when you're not used to it, and a man in my position needs to keep a very clear head. Same with water – fine from wells in my homeland, but water which looks equally pure elsewhere might not suit me. Then there's my people's laws about food – some folk say they're God-given, but I reckon even if they are, they're more to help our health in our climate. I'm usually fine eating whatever the locals do." And he spears a chunk of meat from his stew with relish.

"So what do you eat in your country? Similar to what Egyptians do?"

"Well, we're blessed with quite a choice. Many Hebrews keep sheep or cattle, and of course we harvest corn, grapes – which is where this wine comes from – figs, olives for oil, and so on."

"And do you have celebrations after your harvest, like this?"

Ezra glances around the crowded hall. "Yes, but we tend to run them in together. Like treading the grapes. Of course, it's different when you can rely on the sun staying hot."

"Our weather's not so bad! It's been beautifully fine this week so far."

"If damp," Ezra says doubtfully. "But I suppose you don't get much snow. I remember crossing the mountains on the Mainland, before getting to the coast opposite Britain and getting stuck in a snowdrift. My wife wasn't best pleased. Of course, she was never a keen traveller, even though all our ancestors roamed the desert."

I look quickly at my mother, who's chatting to Jelize – she placed me next to Ezra, as if feeling it too encouraging for her to sit with him – but somehow still has her ears pricked towards our conversation. "You're married, then?"

Ezra takes a drink of his wine. "I haven't been, not for some years now."

"Oh – I'm sorry…"

Ezra stares at me, then lets out a bellow of laughter. "Oh, Rowan, thanks for your sympathy – I've not explained. My wife fell in love with our handsome, heroic rescuer from a mountain tribe. I agreed to divorce her so she could settle down with him."

"That must have been hard!"

"Not really." Ezra draws a piece of linen cloth across his lips. "The marriage was arranged by our parents when we were young. We got on well enough – but no children, and no strong affection. I decided to wait for someone I could care for deeply the second time round." And his gaze flickers towards my mother.

"Well, here we have the chance to choose our own marriage partners. But my mother says you can jump the bonfire in haste with the wrong person, and regret it afterwards."

"Can you remember your father, Rowan?"

"Oh yes. I was only three years old when the accident happened. Of course, he was away from home at the time. He was a kind father, though – always bringing me gifts after his work trips. A cheerful, laughing sort of person – that's how I always think of him."

"Your poor mother! It must have been hard for her to lose such a husband."

"Well, I suppose so," I say doubtfully. Because my memories of my parents together seem to include sudden quarrels, like zigzags of lightning. Which suggest my mother wasn't always as – well, frozen – as she seems now. But I can't be sure.

"So this bonfire-jumping is your form of weddings? No veils for the bride – no processions with music – no religious ceremony?"

It does sound a bit basic, put like that.

"Well, some folk have a priest or priestess give them a blessing. And sometimes the man carries the bride off on his horse, like a pretend abduction or elopement."

Ezra twirls the stem of his goblet and looks gloomily into the lees of the wine. "Your customs sound very energetic. What about older folk who wish to marry?" And he glances again towards my mother.

I try to be helpful. "Um, I suppose you could always build a low bonfire."

"But maybe that wouldn't be thought of as romantic. And what about the family – I take it they must be consulted?"

I look doubtfully at my Uncle Bram at the top table. "I suppose it would be the polite thing to do. Though I can't imagine my – some women – taking much notice."

Ezra follows me in looking at Uncle Bram. "But your mother Raven's – brother by her first marriage, is it? – is quite an important man? I see he and his wife are sitting near some chief at the top table here."

"Yes, and it's all wrong," I say vigorously. "In the temple, we're told we're all equal servants of the Goddess. Just outside, our head people have special seating with an extra firepit at their backs, as well as the central one that does for us all, and they get served first. I expect the Hawk feasting hall and camps north of the Henge have got extra luxuries again."

"Oh, they have. Wonderful wall hangings. Soft feather mattresses. But I can't quibble. They're some of my best customers," Ezra says mildly. "But, to return to marriage – my parents would still think they should have a say in mine. In fact" —he looks endearingly sheepish— "they jumped to the conclusion my wife had perished in the snowstorm. And I thought it simpler to leave it like that."

"So you do have only one wife at a time? I've heard of countries where men don't."

"Well, it varies. Some of our rich and powerful men are polygamous. But it only leads to trouble, in my view. Take my cousin Jacob—"

But I'm fated not to find out about Ezra's cousin, because at that moment some man who seems to be in charge of events stands up, bangs on the top table and gestures for us all to be silent.

"And now we have some entertainment for you," he says. "Four young musicians from our neighbours to the north. We're sure you'll enjoy hearing the Windhawks!"

*

Well, that was brilliant! I realise I'd been expecting spoilt rich boys, having a bit of fun before going back to normal Hawk work (managing lands and ships and 'defensive' war bands), wouldn't be much good at the actual music. But I'm on my feet applauding wildly, as if by instinct. I see a lot of younger folk in the hall are doing the same – among them Beaver Boy, with some of his people; Anyanda will be pleased he's here. She's sitting by Jelize, with her parents being on the top table, and they've not really got much in common. Anyanda always wants Jelize to cast runes to help her track down men, and Jelize says they shouldn't be used for that purpose. But not everyone's as enthusiastic as we are.

"Well," the man on Ezra's other side says rather aggressively, as our chief beckons Kelvan and friends over for a few words, "I could have done without that! Doesn't that harpist lad realise he's meant to sing songs of epic battles, and play music that inspires us to warlike deeds?"

(I did notice that when Kelvan played, especially on his own, he did do quite different pieces from those of the wandering harpers who've come through our village. But he did them well!)

"Excuse me," I say – partly to Ezra, because I'm leaning across him, and partly to the speaker, because we're not meant to contradict our elders, "I thought he was excellent. And why should he play the same songs as everyone else? Sometimes it's good to try a new thing!"

The man looks at me in a bleary fashion. "You young 'uns think you know it all," he growls. "The whole point of a harp player is supporting troops at war."

"But we've not got any big battles going on at the moment," I point out. "It's not like the huge war on the Mainland that Britain got involved in over a hundred years ago. Why shouldn't musicians also make us think about love, friendship, nature, humour, things that are wrong with our society—?"

"Rowan! You sound like my champion."

I've been so involved in saying what I think that I've not realised Kelvan has come up and is standing in front of my place at the table. *He takes my hand and kisses it.* But he's looking amused, so it's probably just a tease, or Hawk high-life manners.

"Well, I'm the champion of certain types of music," I say coolly. Kelvan quirks an eyebrow, as if appreciating the difference. "And it's so silly! Some changes are for the better – or, at least, right for the times."

"Like the original patterns in your weaving?"

"Well, yes." I realise with surprise that Kelvan and I do have something in common. "And with society. Like, if some tribes pay others tribute, are they getting enough in return?" (Like the Hawks, who supposedly protect all Britain from invaders.) "But what you said, too."

"That's good. Because I've been thinking a bit more about the work we could offer you. Would you be interested in a commission to weave completely new garments for future occasions?"

"Well – I think so…"

"Are you free to take a walk with me? We could talk about it more quietly. I'll see you safe back to your people afterwards."

At this point my mother – who must have been listening – stands up and puts a hand to her forehead. "Rowan," she says dramatically, "I feel a little unwell. Will you help me back to our shelter?"

Unwell! My mother's never ill. She's not much good at pretending either. But I don't think she intends to be taken seriously. I can see from Jelize's sceptical expression that it's just an excuse to get me away from the Hawks. Or Kelvan in particular.

Poor old Ezra, however, is quite concerned. "Madam

Raven," he says, bustling up to her. "Allow me to see you to your tent. Two of my men can carry you on a chair if need be."

"That won't be necessary," my mother says crossly, sitting down with a thump.

By now everyone's starting to break into clumps to chat, as those on kitchen duty start clearing away. Beaver Boy comes swaggering up to us.

"Greetings, all," he says, with a flash of his teeth. "Anyanda, Anyasdaughter – I hope you're looking forward to receiving my arrow by tomorrow afternoon."

"If you win, I may. But, for now, I must take my Aunt Raven back to our shelter. She's feeling a little unwell, and my cousin needs to talk about her work to the musicians."

That's rather noble of Anyanda – even if she's trying to show Beaver Boy she's not hanging around waiting for his whistle. I can see my mother practically grinding her teeth. But she can hardly prevent an adult daughter from pursuing her trade, and if she's cut herself off from being part of that, it's her own fault.

"We're sorry Madam Raven's ill. Can I help you escort her?" Crow asks Anyanda eagerly.

"You needn't worry. We'll be fine, thanks."

But Anyanda looks over her shoulder to throw Crow a saucy smile as she takes my mother's arm with exaggerated care and starts to lead her away. Jelize is laughing to herself as she follows them.

The young men all look at each other. I realise it's the first time in my life I've been on my own without any other Dragons about. It's rather a strange feeling.

"Got a kind heart, my girl," Beaver Boy says, rubbing his hands together.

"And would that be Rowan the Weaver's cousin?" asks Kelvan. "She didn't strike me as being anyone's girl."

"Or not one man's in particular," Mart adds.

Beaver Boy shrugs. "Wait till tomorrow! The best at archery usually has his pick."

"But that might not be you," Sparrow points out.

"And another winner might choose a different young woman – like Rowan here," Kelvan says.

"Well, I suppose." Beaver Boy looks at me doubtfully. "But she has got red hair. My people don't think that's very lucky."

(I always thought Bram protected us from being shunned for our unusual lifestyle. Maybe my hair came into it too!)

"They'd have a problem among the Hawks," Kelvan says. "Many of us have red hair."

"Firethorn's hair is much redder than Rowan's," says Sparrow. "Rowan's is pretty – like bronze wire."

I find my tongue. "Who's Firethorn?"

"A girl we all know back home," Crow explains.

"Especially Mart," Sparrow adds.

This time Kelvan, Crow and Sparrow all grin at each other. Mart – who obviously doesn't take jokes well, whatever they mean – glowers at them.

"And," I say to Beaver Boy, getting my voice back, "surely a woman can choose to turn a man down? Whatever contests he wins?"

"Well – you'll see tomorrow." He grins, and saunters back to his people.

Well, I hope he will! Because I've decided: I'm going along with Anyanda's plan.

"Did that Beaver come with you to the festival?" Crow asks wistfully.

"We just met on the way here. We were ambushed by outlaws, only Jelize – that's my foster aunt, who was sitting by Anyanda – talked them out of it."

"You'll have to tell me how she did that," Kelvan says. "I like hearing tales of strategy. Shall we go?" And, as Crow seems about to follow, "Not the rest of you. Just Rowan and I."

Kelvan strides off uphill. There are quite a few people about in the makeshift festival lanes, but mostly heading towards their lower-ground camps. When we've got clear of them, he pauses.

"Why did you——?"

"I wanted to know——"

We've both started speaking at once. A slight feeling of tension slackens as we laugh and walk on.

"You first, Rowan the Weaver," says Kelvan in a courtly manner.

"I just wondered how you came to perform at the westward hall tonight. Are you going round them in turn?"

"Well, hopefully. That's why we wanted to come down to this festival – play to southerners who've not heard us before. I think there'll be other musicians in your hall on other nights."

"I wonder if that argumentative man will prefer them… And you were saying?"

"Oh…just making sure you were happy about weaving us some new clothes when you got home."

"Oh yes. I should be able to fit that in. Do you mean I'd get them sent to you?"

(Sending my wares around the country – not just selling them locally – sounds quite exciting.)

Kelvan shrugs. "You wouldn't need to do that. I can arrange for one of our war bands to collect them next time they're round your way."

Well, that's true. They do travel around the coastal regions on patrol – "eating us out of house and home," as my Aunt Anya puts it, and in this case we all agree with her.

"Or," Kelvan adds, "I could come myself."

I glance at him uncertainly. I may not know many men my own age: Anyanda's brothers, my cousins, are older, and live near the clay works with their wives and families; the boys in the village happen to be a bit younger. I can tell Kelvan doesn't play flirting games in the way Beaver Boy and Anyanda do, but maybe this is a Hawk version of it? I can't see his expression just by starlight – the moon's waning, and the great cressets of fire still burning above our heads throw shadows across his face. I can't get a feel for his thoughts, either.

As I'm wondering about this, I trip on a less well-levelled lump of earth.

"Careful."

Kelvan takes my hand. His is warm and dry. As I hold it, a crackling sensation sweeps up my arm. This won't do! I must be a sensible business woman.

But as I start to say "I can manage", we round a corner and almost bump into two figures which look vaguely familiar. I realise it's two of the Shell men, both still seeming drunk. And now waving cudgels.

I try to say "Sorry" politely and pass by. But they stop dead in front of us.

"Hello, lynx girl – without your lynx," says the one on our right.

The one on Kelvan's left hiccups. "No, she's got the pretty-boy harper. One of those stuck-up swine of Hawks. I reckon we should teach them a bit of respect."

CHAPTER 5

But even as he's speaking, Kelvan's thrust his harp into my hands, muttering, "Hold this," and jumped between them. Now, in a lightning flash, he's somehow managing to trip the left-hand (drunker) one from behind, so he's now sprawling face upwards, the cudgel flying out of his hand. And Kelvan's now kneeling at his far side, holding what looks like a small, sharp knife to the other man's throat.

"All right, ugly boy," he says quite lightly to the other Shell person (to my surprise, hardly even sounding out of breath), "if you want to save your friend's life, give the lady your weapon. Now."

The other Shell man seems quite taken aback by all this happening so swiftly. But he hands me his cudgel. What with that, and the harp – which is small but heavy – I'm starting to feel like a pack animal. Kelvan still holds the knife out as he rises and picks up the other one.

"All right," the Shell man says, "you've won. For now."

He doesn't sound that angry. If anything, he's slightly respectful.

"Swear by the powers of the Goddess that you won't follow us."

"Oh yes. I swear. I'll have to get him back anyway.

When he's come round a bit."

We all look at the man sprawled on the ground.

"Did you knock him out of his senses?" I ask Kelvan.

"No need – the drink's done that."

"Well, have your harp back. We'd better turn him on his side or he might choke."

"If you must," Kelvan shrugs.

"You'd best lend a hand," I tell the other Shell man sharply. "He'll be like a dead weight. I can't move him on my own."

We roll the unconscious man on his side while Kelvan observes us from a little way uphill.

The friend sits back on his heels, pushing his rather shaggy hair out of his eyes. He seems to be sobering up. "Thanks, lynx girl. That was a kind action."

"Well, it's what any decent person would do. And my name's Rowan."

"I'm not sure everyone would agree with you – Rowan. Not in the circumstances."

"If you'll be all right with him now, I'd better go."

"Yes, fine. But just one thing – aren't you a Dragon?"

"That's right. Why?"

"Just wondered what you're doing running around with a Hawk. Everyone knows Hawks aren't kind."

"Can we talk here? Kezzie's coming to look for me, so if we sit on the grass she'll find us faster than if we're walking about." And I sit down on a little plateau not far from the base of the temple.

"Like a moving target? Yes, that's all right with me," Kelvan says cheerfully as he joins me. "Does Kezzie usually come looking for you at this time of night?"

"She's running to find me because she can tell I've been in a bit of danger."

"She knows from a distance?"

"Well, we don't talk to each other in human language, so it's not much different."

"And can you do that with people too? Talk to them in the same way?"

"Not so much. Like with my cousin – we have to scry if we're not meeting in person."

"I wondered because my mother's a bit that way. A lot of folk are, in the Green Isle. But even there, they say you're more likely to have those sort of talents if you're the seventh child of a seventh child. I'm only a second son of a second son, so that lets me out! Although my father's elder brother's a priest and astronomer. So he does that sort of thing in a different way. He and his wife – she's gone to Spirit" —he makes the appropriate gesture— "had no children. Which didn't impress my grandfather. So he said if my uncle wanted to become a priest after he was widowed, he might as well."

"So he won't be king after your grandfather?"

"No. It goes by election, anyhow."

"But I thought the Council chose a descendant of the last king, if there was one."

"Well, sometimes," Kelvan says, his voice like silk over ice, "the Council has to think again."

Goodness! This seems a difficult topic. Maybe I'd better change the subject.

"When you asked the Shell person to swear by the Goddess – do you believe that makes a difference?"

"I'm sure he believes it. That's what counts."

"And you're not like your mother? I mean, you never have any clear-seeing moments yourself?"

"No," Kelvan says, quite cheerfully, "not at all. Although I can see it's a useful thing to be able to do – when you can trust it."

"Oh." I can't help being a bit disappointed. "So you've

not had a recent picture of two halves of a shell closing together?"

Kelvan laughs. "No, Rowan the Weaver, I haven't. And if this was your warning to beware of the Shell tribe, it didn't really help us, did it? What was handy was there only being two of them. I could've managed three if you helped."

"I would have! You were the one who gave me your harp to hold!"

"Well, that was important – wasn't it, my beauty?" Kelvan adds to his harp as he softly plucks at the strings. "I just meant – more than three, we'd've been better off making a run for it."

"Yes, yes, we would."

I'm a bit taken aback at Kelvan admitting this. I'm sure the younger men from our village – or Beaver Boy and his friends – or even Kelvan's fellow-musicians – would have insisted they were capable of taking on ten men from another tribe single-handed. And some of them might even be silly enough to try.

"You sound a bit surprised," Kelvan comments. I realise that, in an ordinary way, he does notice things about people. "Do you think I should have been ready to fight a whole bunch of them – no matter what happened to us as a result?"

"No, of course not. I just didn't expect you to be so sensible. Most men aren't."

"Most people aren't—" Kelvan begins.

Then I shriek with delight as Kezzie bounds up to us, and I fling my arms around her, burying my face in her warm, calming fur. After we've greeted each other, I send her a couple of thought pictures of what's happened in the feasting hall. I feel she already knows about the recent danger we've overcome. Then she rubs herself up against Kelvan, and he strokes her too. I'm a bit surprised on what good terms they are already. But I think I like it.

"Well, I suppose I'd best see you safely back to your family – even though I'm sure you'd be fine with Kezzie. Your mother didn't seem too happy about your going off with me."

So he'd noticed that too.

"It's not you personally," I explain, as we start heading westward down the slope. "It's any Hawks. Even though…" I pause, not sure what to say next.

"Even though she's one of us?"

"You could tell?"

Kelvan shrugs again. "Think I've heard her brothers talk about her. Their widowed sister Raven, who lives down in the south-west with her Dragon family by marriage. And her child."

So maybe I've got uncles I've never met. But—

"If they mean me, I'm not a child!"

"It sounds as if they've not seen you since you were a baby. So they wouldn't realise you're a woman now."

"Do you know them well, then?"

"They and their wives are friends of my parents. They're our local master builders. I wonder why your mother's never told you about them."

"I wonder if they ever worked with my father," I say, excited. "He restored henges. That's how he had his accident – in a fall. And he designed structures, too. There's a big wooden bridge he invented, to go over the marshy ground a bit south of us. Arvan's Walkway, it's called. Did your – my uncles – ever mention him?"

"Well, not that I've ever heard. Not at all." A pause. "Tell me," Kelvan says, "how did you train to be a weaver – beyond the basics all women know? I take it you didn't go away for years, like we did with Warrior School?"

"Or Jelize with training to be a priestess – when she was going to be one. I learned quite a lot from an older woman in our village – she's gone to Spirit now" —we bend our heads and make the appropriate hand gesture— "and now and then there were special Sun's Day workshops for our local settlements, with two experts – a man and a woman – my Uncle Bram allowed me time off from archery practice to attend."

"They taught you well. Is that how you've come to do these designs which are different from everyone else's?"

"Oh, no one taught me," I say, a bit surprised. "I do that out of my head."

"Ah," Kelvan says, with sympathetic interest, "a bit like me making up songs!"

"And us wanting to go to festivals with what we do!"

"Yes… You know, we've got an even better place for them really far north. It's where some of the first farming was done in Britain."

"If you say so," I agree politely.

"We're hoping to be back for the winter solstice. You'd like it there, Rowan…"

"Well, maybe I would."

I'm hoping this will lead to some suggestion as to how I could get there. But instead Kelvan starts talking about some plant up there that can be used both as candles and for brewing. He may not be too keen on his grandfather, but he seems very attached to his tribal homeland!

"Some people even say they've seen a unicorn there."

"What's that?"

"A horse with a single horn growing out of its forehead. The totem animal for all North Britain. The Hawk is just for my tribe." (The boss tribe, of course. And I'm not surprised that even the horses are fancier up north.)

"So it – they – live up there?"

"They're not supposed to live in our world at all. Just sometimes turn up in it."

"Oh – like us with dragons!"

Kelvan smiles. "Could be just a wild horse seen by a beer-fuelled imagination. Same as the water-horses which are meant to live in our lochs. I do plenty of swimming, and I've never seen one!"

"Oh – that's good," I say, though I'm a bit doubtful about Kelvan's sceptical attitude. "Anyway, there's my shelter – the one just below us."

"Fine! I'll be seeing you, Rowan!"

Kelvan turns with an airy wave, and starts making his way back uphill. I see three figures emerge from some bushes higher up the path. And even before voices drift to me downwind, I recognise them. Square build, with square-cut hair – Mart. Slight build, longer hair – Sparrow. Tall and thin – Crow. So Kelvan's bandmates have tracked him and come to meet him. I had wondered if he'd try to kiss me goodnight. So it's a good thing he didn't. I suppose.

"Well?" Anyanda bounces up eagerly as Kezzie and I enter our shelter. "How did it go?"

(The older women are all snoring softly. So much for their arguments – or concern for my welfare.)

I slump wearily onto my own blankets. "Oh, good. I think I've lined up some further sales."

"And what *else*?"

"Well, we got set on by a couple of those Shell characters. But Kelvan fought them off."

Anyanda clasps her hands.

"He saved you! How romantic!"

"Well, I don't think he wanted either of us to get beaten up. But he was more concerned about his harp than anything else."

Now Anyanda frowns. "So what *did* you talk about? Apart from sales?"

"Oh, lots of things. Religion. Politics. Families. It turns

out my mother's got two brothers who are friends of his parents. Just fancy."

"Well, if that's the sort of thing you both enjoy. I reckon Gerwas" —oh, yes, that's Beaver Boy's real name— "and I could have made better use of our time." She adds, in a small voice, "Did he stay long at the banquet? After I'd left."

I cast my mind back. "Not long. But I'll tell you one thing. I've been thinking about your plan for me to go in for the archery contest. And I'm sure now that it's a great idea!"

CHAPTER 6

"Oh, Rowan." Anyanda heaves a sigh of bliss. "This has been the most wonderful morning ever. So much trade…and almost all with young men. I'm so glad I persuaded my father you'd need my help with selling from your stall."

It's true that, from Anyanda's viewpoint, this must be like heaven – and if it's true there are different levels of heaven (something even priests and priestesses argue about), this must be her idea of one of the highest.

When we set up our stall, we didn't expect many customers to begin with, what with it being a clear, cold, rain-washed sort of morning, and most adults recovering from the heavy eating and drinking of First Feast Night. But just when we were rolling out tunics and hanging up cloaks, our bodyguard – the youngest one, whom Ezra hired in this country to practise speaking British with – came up, realising he wanted a warmer pair of trousers than any he's brought from home. He said Ezra pays well, so he insisted on paying us too. Then, as we finished sorting him out, up came two young men, who stopped in front of our stall. One nudged the other, who said – not looking me quite in the eye –

"My mate reckons you saved my life last night. So – uh – thanks."

I realised it was the two Shell men from last night. But they looked quite ordinary by morning light, not scary or figures of fun. Of course, I'd never seen them sober before.

"And," the speaker went on, "I've brought you this."

He pulled out the most magnificent whorled shell, already on a leather necklace, and handed it to me with quite a courtly gesture. It's like the one I already wear, which is meant to record your thoughts, but in any case makes a good ornament. But I'd never seen such a good specimen before.

"I can't take this!" I told him.

"Why not?" (He sounded a bit huffy.)

"Because it's too good. I bet you could buy – um – lots of things with it back home. At least let me give you something in return. After all, all I did was to say to your friend we should turn you on your side."

"And stopped your Hawk boyfriend from slitting my throat."

"I don't think he'd have done that anyway."

"Your tribe doesn't have them for neighbours like we do. Don't trust 'em."

The shell-giver's friend frowns at him, as if he really thinks there's something going on between me and Kelvan, and they should be tactful. "Although some of them may not be too bad close up and on their own," he says.

"Well, maybe they're not so bad with you Beaker folk—"

"Dragons," Anyanda muttered – sometimes people call us Beakers because we make them, but that's not really correct.

"—and we can give them as good as we get when it comes to ordinary border raids. It's more the way they don't give us any respect."

"Yes, I can see that must be a bit annoying," I agreed, rather feebly. But I did understand how trying it must be. "Anyway, gentlemen, you must choose some little gift each, if you really want me to take this lovely shell."

After they'd gone on their way, with a neck warmer each, we had a bit of general custom. Then who should turn up but Kelvan and company? After general greetings, Kelvan said, "That's a beautiful shell you're wearing, Rowan."

"Yes, one of the Shell men gave it to me. A sort of – uh – apology for last night."

Kelvan raised his eyebrows. "Pretty civilised behaviour for one of them." But he said it in an amused-sounding way. Anyanda threw him a disappointed look, as if she thought he should have turned green with jealousy.

"They're quite nice when you get to know them. Same as most of us really, I suppose."

Mart looked at me approvingly. "You see!" he told Kelvan. "I always said we should take the trouble to make friends of them. They'd be useful allies."

Kelvan shrugged. "Maybe we can discuss it after the festival. We need to concentrate on our music for now. Speaking of which, we can fit in a bit of practice before noon."

"You're going to the archery contest, though?" Anyanda asked.

"Yes – got to cheer Sparrow on."

"So you're going in for the competition too?" I asked Sparrow, thinking if one of them were keen on archery, it made sense it was their string player.

"Yes, and he's good." Mart, who seemed in a better mood today, answered for Sparrow, clapping him on the back.

"Probably not in competition with a good part of Britain," Sparrow said modestly. "Your Beaver friend seemed pretty confident about his chances."

Anyanda and I couldn't stop ourselves from looking at each other and laughing. But of course the Hawks thought this was just something about her and Beaver Boy.

"At least this morning's team games will be over," I said, to change the subject. "Like that silly one where the teams try to kick a dead animal's bladder between opposite posts. Do you have that back home?"

Kelvan grinned. "We have one you'd probably think even sillier. We hit small balls with sticks, to get them past each other's teams."

"And," Mart added, "there's the especially stupid one where we hit the balls into holes in the ground."

"Or, in your case, not," Crow grinned.

Mart laughed. "Definitely not, in my case."

Goodness, what had come over him? It's true a shaft of pale sunlight had come out, striking across his face. But he seemed more lit up from the inside.

After I'd watched him walking off with Kelvan, arms around each other's shoulders blood-brother fashion, I couldn't resist saying to Crow and Sparrow, "What's happened to Mart? He seems – um – different today."

"More cheerful?" Sparrow suggested. "He would be. He's had a message."

"From that Firethorn girl?" (I could see by the way the two men glanced at each other that my guess had hit the target.) "Did she scry him?"

"No, one of Kelvan's father's men rode in last night," Crow explained.

Of course – the better-off Hawks would have people riding around who could deliver messages for them.

"Anyway, we'd better go," Sparrow said, looking to where Kelvan was beckoning.

"Yes. His Highness calls," said Crow.

"Kelvan's not like that – using his rank. He's just a natural leader," Sparrow protested, to us as well as Crow.

But, whatever he may be, they went off, and walking pretty fast too.

Then we got a batch of beaker-makers, a few young single men who'd been given a holiday by Anyanda's brothers. They said they'd been asked to look us up and make sure we were getting on all right. But they stayed for a while, buying several items of clothing, and I said a quick prayer of thanks for the cold snap aiding trade. They seemed a lot keener on talking to us than they'd been whenever we met under our parents' eyes, too!

Before they'd quite drifted away, Beaver Boy swaggered up with a couple of friends. "I hope you're packing up in good time," he said to Anyanda, with a flash of his bold, dark eyes. "You need to get a front seat for the contest. Ready for me to present you with my arrow at the end."

Anyanda dimpled at him, as if taking him seriously. And maybe at some level she was. "Rowan and I can't wait."

So we're packing up, having already sent Ezra's servant off with some of our heavier stuff, and I've agreed with Kezzie that she'll meet up with us in the archery field. Well, Anyanda really. Kezzie understands she can't show she knows me. I think. Anyanda mutters "Aunt Raven" to me, and I see my mother marching down our alley (she can manage to carry all her wares in two big baskets, one on each arm, lucky her) and come to a stop in front of us. Now, there's a nuisance. Because if she sticks with us for the afternoon, how will I get a chance to change into my disguise? Although, the Goddess be thanked, I've obviously got spare trousers with me – and caps.

"People are talking about you two," she addresses us, without so much as a 'good-day, daughter' or 'how's it going, niece?'

Anyanda looks delighted. "Are they?" she asks eagerly. "Well, we have made a lot of sales this morning."

My mother frowns. "Yes, and how have you made them? I heard two young men telling a friend, 'You've got to go to the weavers' stall with the two girls. Some of the designs are a bit unusual' – you see, Rowan, I did warn you – 'but the women are worth seeing!' Then the other one said, 'Yes, there's a dark one with a great figure, and a bronze-haired one who's quite fun to talk to. You'll have a good time there.'"

Anyanda's honestly bewildered. "But that's good! If that's what they're saying, we'll get more customers."

My mother sniffs. "Customers for what, I ask!"

"Oh, Aunt Raven! There's nothing wrong in finding different ways to attract people to your stall. Maybe Rowan and I can advise you on it."

(Directions to the haughtiest herbalist at the festival? I can just imagine it.)

My mother laughs. She does let her human side loose at times. "I'll think about it, Anyanda," she says, and walks on.

"I wish Aunt Raven would let us help her," Anyanda says seriously as we follow her. "I don't suppose she'll tell us any more about those young men she overheard, either."

"No, I am a bit curious," I admit. "Though I'm sure they weren't Hawks, or she'd have been twice as cross."

"She's so strange about that. Especially when you think she is a Hawk."

"Yes, and from what Kelvan was telling me, these brothers of hers up north are pretty famous builders – same as my father was. They're friends of his parents, even."

Anyanda's eyes widen. "Your mother's well connected, then. I'm glad she stayed here, so we could be friends. But why in the Goddess's name didn't she go back to her own tribe, after your father's accident?"

"You truly don't know?"

Anyanda shakes her head so hard her dark curls fly about wildly. "No. My parents never talk about it. You know I'd have told you if they did."

(I'm sure that's true. Anyanda's an excellent gossip.)

She continues, "Of course, some of our tribe are prejudiced against Hawks, so maybe that's one reason why they don't mention it. Though I don't know why everyone carries on as if they're all high and mighty. The musicians aren't like that."

"No-o," I agree rather doubtfully. "Though I still feel there's a sort of edge to them. As if they think deep down that they're better than anyone who isn't a Hawk."

"They weren't like that when they were talking about their games," Anyanda protests.

"All right, they were quite funny then... Kelvan was telling me more about their sports on the way home last night. They like swimming in icy lakes. Sometimes they'll build a fire at the side, run to it to warm up and dry off, and then jump in the lake again. Kelvan says it gives you a great feeling. Though I think maybe it only does that if you've grown up with it."

Anyanda's eyes brighten. "We're not far from a big river here. Why don't you suggest they go swimming in that?"

"Um – because at this time of year the sea-tides affect it, so it gets muddy and very dangerous?"

"You are a spoilsport," Anyanda pouts. "We could have seen them stripping. Mind you, Kelvan's a bit thin."

"He's got very good muscles, as it happens. I noticed that last night."

"Of course, you're a bit on the skinny side yourself. If you were to mate, I reckon you'd have thin babies."

Honestly! Sometimes I can see my mother's point about Anyanda.

"He's just a business contact," I say through gritted teeth. "Who happens to be quite a friendly one."

"You needn't get in a huff. I mean, make him jump the bonfire with you first."

"I'm not here to make anyone do that. Or get married at all. And don't let my mother hear you say that. You know she's only allowed me to come if it's just about trade."

"Aunt Raven? It's like cauldrons calling pots black, her complaining about us. Look how she lets Ezra do her favours because he's taken a liking to her. It's embarrassing in older people."

"Not if it makes them happy. Kelvan was saying his parents' marriage was a political one, but they fell in love, and are to this day."

"For someone you just see on business," Anyanda jeers, "you do take a lot of notice of what Kelvan says."

(Instead of listening to her. She doesn't like that.)

We glare at each other, and for a moment I think we're going to go back to childhood, when our quarrels often ended in mud fights. But then I think of a more adult weapon.

"Anyanda," I say sternly, "you want me to take part in this afternoon's competition, don't you?"

"You're not going to back out?"

"And have a chance of winning?"

"Of course!"

Anyanda's staring at me – she's not used to me sticking up for myself like this.

"Well, then. You need to keep me calm. And you need to think of ways to distract my mother while I'm sorting out my disguise."

CHAPTER 7

"A bit nerve-wracking, isn't it? All this waiting about?"

I nod, and point to my neck, swathed in one of my own warmers. A sore throat, due to some slight infection, is my excuse for only speaking in a whispery croak, or not at all.

There are only about twenty of us going in for the archery contest. I guess most people wouldn't try unless they knew they were the best in their part of Britain. Because who wants to look foolish in front of a huge crowd made up of several tribes? I'm also thinking: if it's true there's a difference between male and female energy which some folk can sense, it's a good thing no one here can – though that may be because they're all so busy retesting bowstrings, checking arrows and feeling the direction of the wind: it blocks out anything else.

"Of course, it's fair enough in a way," the speaker adds. "Best of three shots from three groups, and one of each group going forward to the final. D'you reckon that's because three's a special sort of number? Like it's a religious thing? Or just what the stewards think's most practical?"

This time I shake my head to show I've no idea. Which I haven't. My neighbour-in-line (whom I vaguely recognise as a clay-worker) is plainly quite a talkative person – unless that's just due to nerves. He goes on, "Bit strange how they've mixed us up, though. I'd've thought they'd keep us more to our own tribes."

Yes, I've noticed, and I think this is a good thing. The competition should be about the individual's skill and not tribal rivalries. However, I've also seen Beaver Boy (Gerwas) and Sparrow have ended up in different groups from me, the Goddess be praised!

The clay-worker continues. "And all this argument about what sort of moving target to have for the three in the final! You know we were going to have birds, only the Hawks objected to killing them for sport – as if it was some kind of insult to themselves."

As I object to killing living things for sport anyway, the same as Jelize does, this is one case where I'm glad the Hawks have so much influence. I start to say something, as huskily as I can, about being quite happy to shoot at small balls hurled from large catapults. But – and maybe it's a good thing, before I risk speaking too strongly – one of the stewards is calling for silence. And as soon as he's got it, apart from the odd mutterings you're bound to get with any group of people, the first names are called. And we begin.

This is going brilliantly! The weather's changed to a hazy sky (better than dazzling sun, at least) and a light wind which is veering around, coming and going with odd gusts in an off-putting way. But I know I'm shooting at the top of my form, and I think I know why. It's because I'm not shooting as Rowan the Weaver but as the mysterious Mab from the Mountains. The others have all got family and friends shouting for them, as they're allowed to do between turns. And if I were really Mab, someone from the far west without anyone to cheer for him, it might feel a bit lonely. Only, as it is, I'm like a person in one of those countries where they do whole plays pretending to be someone else, not just in ballads or as part of temple rituals. Except this is better again, because if you're an actor who goes wrong, people who know you in real life might remember. But Mab can just melt back invisibly into his mountain mists once the competition's over, however he's done.

Of course, as we're all wearing short tunics, everyone can see my dragon tattoo. But most Dragons in the crowd are focusing on archers they know. The only ones bothered about me are Anyanda and Kezzie; and, of course, they have to pretend not to be. Kezzie's making a much better job of it than Anyanda, though – I can see out of the corner of my eye how she's pulling Anyanda by her skirt to stop her waving when I'm about to shoot.

The competition is pretty well organised, at that. We've got boards nailed up with different colours painted on them. Red's the innermost one, and so far I've hit it twice. But so have a couple of the others in my group. I'm feeling alert and cheerful at the same time – it's one of those days when you know your arrow will go where you send it. So I'm not surprised that now I've scored red for the third time. One other archer does too, and the stewards have to look closely at the board. But then they call, "Mab from the Mountains, step forward!" And I can see they've decided my arrow's nearer the centre.

There's a bit of a pause while everyone watching can move around – snack, talk, relieve themselves – whatever they want to do, really. I can see most of the losers are joining them, which shows a good spirit on their part, though a couple are slinking off in a gloomy sort of way.

The steward who memorised my name earlier beckons me to join the other two finalists. I'm dismayed, but not surprised, to see Beaver Boy is one. And, guess what, Sparrow(hawk) is the other. Only the two young men most likely to recognise me out of all the other archers!

"Well," Beaver Boy grins at me and Sparrow, "may the best man win. Which, of course, should be me."

I can tell he's saying that on purpose to put us off – it's not just his usual bigheadedness. He looks overheated, though. I can't help congratulating myself that I can weave clothes which can be reasonably light – his tunic looks a bit matted to my trained eye. And his attitude makes me keener than ever on trying to beat him. Sparrow, however, looks a bit taken aback.

"Well," he says, with a nod to me, "our Dragon friend here may surprise us."

Then he looks at me more closely.

"Have you got any family here? You look a bit like a new friend we've made at the festival, a nice girl called Rowan, who's a weaver. She's a Dragon too."

Well, at least he's saying good things about me! I gesture violently at my throat with my spare hand (Beaver Boy moves hastily away, as if not wanting to catch anything) and I spread my arms wide, as if to say 'I've no idea'.

Sparrow actually seems satisfied with that. Maybe Hawks would think it's just a general Dragon likeness. He goes on to say, "If you don't know anyone here, you're welcome to join me and my friends for tonight's feast. We're musicians, so we move around the halls. But we're in our own, the North one, tonight."

I'm so touched, I feel a lump come in my supposedly poorly throat. This proves some Hawks can be kind. Although, unfortunately, it doesn't say anything about Kelvan, who I don't imagine minds if Sparrow asks some stranger in; but I'm not sure he'd bother if it was left to him.

This shooting at a moving target is certainly a lot tougher than what we did earlier. First time round, we all miss, as we're getting our eye in. We're shooting in turn still – first Beaver Boy, then Mab/me, then Sparrow. I think this reflects our rankings with the non-moving targets, which means Beaver Boy has done best so far. I feel sorry for Sparrow, shooting third, although I suppose it gives him chance to learn from our mistakes. The atmosphere around us is really tense now, taut like our bowstrings. Even as Mab, I can feel it. And Sparrow turns out to be very unlucky. Because Beaver Boy and I have both hit the target with no trouble this second time. But Sparrow's arrow – which seems to fly as true as ours – is taken by a sudden gust of wind, and veers so sharply it almost hits one of the stewards. He jumps away as the arrow skims his shoulder.

The stewards, who are also our judges, all get together in a huddle. The crowd really is silent now. Beaver Boy grins at me as if to say 'that's our rival out of the way'. But I feel sorry for Sparrow, who's looking glum. I start to say something reassuring, and quickly turn it into a cough. Then the head steward approaches us, looking stern. But he is a priest in ordinary life, whereas the others are regular festivalgoers, men who've done this before. So maybe he often looks like that.

"The Goddess be with you all," he begins, just as a polite greeting. "You've all shown impressive skills. But you, young man" —looking at Sparrow— "I'm afraid, after that last shot, we'll have to disqualify you."

Sparrow looks as if he's expected no less. But now we have a sudden interruption, as Kelvan bounds up to arrive among us. (He's been on the far side from my first group, with a lot of Hawks. Being Mab helped me not to take too much notice of him.)

"Are you telling Sparrowhawk he's no longer in the contest?" he demands of the priest. "Because if so, that's unfair. He was unlucky with the change in wind direction.

It doesn't prove anything about his ability as an archer compared with the others."

"My son – Prince Kelvan," the priest begins. He seems to be switching between a temple style of address, where we're all sons and daughters of the Goddess, to the outside world, where rank and wealth matter. (Come to that, with Kelvan's uncle being a High Priest up north, maybe he outranks everyone all round.) But, to be fair to the priest, he continues quite firmly, "I appreciate the wind change was unfortunate for your friend and tribal brother. But some of my fellow judges feel that in itself shows that his winning would be displeasing to the Goddess."

"Yes, the man his arrow clipped is saying that, I guess. Isn't that just bearing a grudge, which would surely displease Her?"

"Thanks, Kelvan," Sparrow says with determination, "but our holy brother is right. Our Beaver friend and this gentleman from the far west are better archers than I am. After all, they scored more reds at the start. So I accept the judges' verdict."

The priest's face lights up. I can tell he's a decent man who really approves of Sparrow. Not just because Sparrow's saved him from a confrontation with Kelvan, either. "You show true humility, my son," he says, raising his hand in a blessing. "May the Goddess reward you for it."

Sparrow turns pink beneath his freckles, but in a pleased way. Kelvan shrugs. "Maybe you should have contests for being humble," he says lightly. "Except folk like Sparrowhawk would keep insisting someone else should win."

"Not your sort of competition, I think, Prince Kelvan."

"No," Kelvan says cheerfully, "and I thank the Goddess for it."

The priest shakes his head, but smiles. "Well, I dare say all have different gifts to offer Her. But may She light you on your path too." He raises his hand in a blessing, which Kelvan acknowledges, then, as we watch him, walks back to the area dominated by Hawks.

"Well" —the priest turns to me and Beaver Boy— "it's between you, Gerwas – I remember you from last year – and our visitor from further west. Now, for the last round of this contest, someone will again release a ball from the catapult. But this time you shoot together."

I can't help feeling a bit distracted by Kelvan's intervention. It certainly showed Sparrow in a good light. And Kelvan, to an extent, because he did try to help a friend and have justice done – as he saw it – and he accepted the priest's rather critical words with good humour. But I can't help wondering what Kelvan's own real take on religion is; plus, however foolishly, I can't help feeling a bit annoyed he just accepted me as Mab without a second glance.

As I shake my head to clear it of these thoughts, buzzing around like bees in a hive, the priest looks slightly concerned. "I understand you're suffering from some sort of ailment of the throat," he tells me. "It doesn't seem to have impaired your shooting, but maybe you should see a herbalist when this is over. Have you come across any here?"

Well, I certainly have. For a moment, I start to laugh wildly, but turn it into a choking fit. Then when offered a drink, I brush it aside and nod to show I'm ready to continue. Because – thanks to nearly giving myself away having settled me down again – I really am.

As the ball flies in the air, I see Gerwas aiming to hit it at the top of its arc. I give him one heartbeat before I loose my own arrow. It follows his, splitting it down the middle, and soars on to embed itself in the ball.

Everyone in the field goes a bit mad. They're shrieking things like "Good shot, Mab" and "Well done, Westerner." I can hardly believe I've done it myself.

I feel a dazed grin coming over my face as I slowly raise my bow above my head, champion-wise. Beaver Boy comes closer, and for a moment I'm worried as to what he'll do or say. But he's actually beaming, and thumps me on the shoulder – a bit hard, but I can tell he means well.

"That was a brilliant shot, man. Even better than I could do. I'm impressed!"

I'm starting to realise a bit more what Anyanda sees in Beaver Boy. He can obviously be generous-spirited. And, I suddenly understand, he's one of those true sportspeople who are happy to see a game well played, whoever wins or loses.

And now Anyanda comes running up, and hugs me, Kezzie close behind her. "Rowan, Rowan! You did it!" she screams. She begins to jump me up and down in an improvised dance. Which knocks my cap sideways. And my hair, which was skewered to it from inside, comes loose. And – longer than that of any man present – it cascades wildly down my back.

CHAPTER 8

"Well, that's both of us disqualified," Sparrow says quite cheerfully as we lie in the long grass of a hill above the contest field, Kezzie and Snapper beside us. "At least now we can relax and enjoy the autumn sun. It's a shame about you, though, Rowan. I mean, you deserved to win."

"Well, overall I guess Gerwas was the best. And I had broken one of their rules, even if I think it's a silly one. The head judge – the priest – he was quite nice about it, though. He even seemed to think it was quite funny. I suppose he thought it was just a young person's prank."

"Wasn't it, then? Did you want to prove something about women being as good at archery as men?"

"Well, that came into it," I say, chewing thoughtfully on a blade of grass. "But of course it all started with Anyanda being so eager for me to do it."

"Anyanda! But she seemed happy enough to accept Gerwas's arrow at the end. Why would she want him to lose?"

"Oh – something to do with her being keen on him but him taking her for granted. I think."

Sparrow purses his lips. "Poor Crow!"

I'm surprised. "What's Crow got to do with it?"

"He's been pretty taken with your cousin. Talked about asking her parents if they'd agree to a marriage."

"What, without asking her first if she liked the idea?"

"Well – it's the traditional way."

"That doesn't mean it's a good way. And I expect it was only because he was nervous she wouldn't accept him."

"Maybe. Not very confident, Crow isn't."

"And what about the Windhawk pact – that none of you are going to settle down with a girl until after you've done your year's travelling?"

"Maybe Crow thought he could come back for your cousin when the year was up." (Or maybe he didn't think it through at all.) "But it doesn't matter now. Not after she's taken Gerwas's arrow in public."

"So is that like saying she'll be willing to jump the bonfire with him?"

"Well, possibly... There's a sort of symbolism about a woman accepting the winner's arrow in these sorts of competitions. About male and female relations. I think that's why there's a tradition of the contests being male only."

I think I see what Sparrow means. "So there's no one you'd have given the arrow to?"

"Oh – no girl in my life!" Sparrow says in a hurried sort of way. "But I only entered for fun. I'm not like you and Kelvan – the sort of people who bother to be good at whatever they undertake."

I've not really thought of myself like that before, but I can see Sparrow's point. Even if it makes me sound rather boring. And it makes me realise why I get irritated by my mother's attitude to her herbalism. She does it in such a workaday way, just happy to concoct and sell the most common remedies. I know now she wasn't brought up to have a trade – but she could still make so much more of it!

"Although," Sparrow goes on, "I don't think you're the sort of person who just likes winning for the sake of it."

"What about Kelvan?"

Sparrow considers this.

"He's just used to winning things. I think he'd be surprised not to," he says finally. "Of course, us Hawks – even ones who aren't like Kelvan, of noble blood – we're expected to excel at something. Whether we want to or not. And all of us, including women, to have some warrior training."

"But you don't enjoy that?"

"Well," Sparrow says cautiously, "the friendship with your blood brothers – that's good. And how me, Kelvan, Crow and Mart started playing together."

I roll on my back and stare at the sky, which is that deep blue that dyers can never quite get right in fabrics. Kezzie and Snapper are now asleep. "Is the music what you care most about?"

"Well, that's more for fun too. I mean, I love it – but it's not all-important to me like it is to Kelvan."

I sit up so I can look at him seriously. "So what do you want to be? I mean, after your festival-travelling year? A landowner?"

Sparrow sits up too. "No, a weather-teller. I think I've got a feel for it," he says, holding up one finger to the wind. "But not just an ordinary one. One that travels in other countries, to see how they manage crops, buildings and so on, in different kinds of weathers. Do you know, Rowan" —his eyes sparkle— "there are countries on the Mainland, nearer the Middle Sea, where mountains actually throw out fire from their summits. Only not all the time, I don't think."

"I bet you just want an excuse to go and see them! And it does sound exciting. But will your temple pay for you to do that?"

"They might – when I explain it's to find ideas which could work over here. But in any case, my eldest sister – the one I share Snapper with – she's marrying someone who'll help take over running the estate. So my parents will help me out. They can see it's something I really want to do."

(I might have known money wouldn't be a problem.)

"Why do you call him Snapper, anyway? He's not at all a snappy sort of dog."

"He snaps things up if you leave them lying around. Not just food – could be brooches – anything, really." Sparrow pulls Snapper's ears fondly as he adds. "We have tried to teach him – and my sister can be pretty firm – he's just completely untrainable in that way."

I think Sparrow's attitude – happy his dog's just a mischievous pet, not a working dog – is rather nice. "You know," I can't help saying, "you don't seem to me like the usual sort of Hawk." I add hastily, "I mean that in a good way."

"You do?" Sparrow seems pleased but embarrassed. "But I thought you and Kelvan, um…"

I feel my eyes narrowing, and Kezzie stirs. "Me and Kelvan what?"

"Oh, nothing. I mean, it's just as well if you're not interested. Considering Firethorn and everything."

"What about this Firethorn? You were the one who said Mart had a special liking for her. Doesn't she feel the same?"

"Well – it's complicated."

(I've noticed folk usually say that when they don't want to explain something.)

"Are you saying Firethorn prefers Kelvan?" I ask boldly.

Sparrow sighs. "I think she really likes Mart. But she also likes the idea of being a queen. And with Kelvan's grandfather recommending the Council of the North name him as successor, to marry Kelvan would give her a good chance of it."

I can't help remembering what Kelvan said about the Council. "Does Kelvan want to be a king, though?"

"It would be made hard for him to refuse. His grandfather would see to that."

"All right. But even if he were king, couldn't he still choose the person he wanted to marry? Are you saying that would be Firethorn?"

"No. But she might choose him."

"Against his wishes? I can't believe that."

"Well, not exactly. But when Kelvan gets wrapped up in his music," Sparrow says rather sadly, "he doesn't seem to notice other people very much. And, of course, he's known Firethorn all his life. Well, we all have – tribal meetings, warrior training ceremonies families can attend, naming ceremonies, weddings, funerals – plus her father's lands run alongside Kelvan's father's. So you see…"

"That she could easily get a marriage arranged, and he'd just put up with it?"

"Something like that." Sparrow looks at me intently. "I wish you and he were together, though, Rowan. You're much nicer than Firethorn."

(I wonder for a moment if Sparrow's interested in me in that way himself. But somehow I know it's not that – and, of course, he wouldn't push Kelvan at me if he were.)

"Well," I say lightly, "I'm not sure if he's nice enough for me."

And despite Sparrow's horrified face – and the picture of a shell starting to close at the back of my own mind – I know I've spoken the truth.

Then Kezzie and Snapper both sit up alertly on their haunches as if they can see – or smell – someone approaching. As I shade my eyes, I can see a solitary figure climbing the hill towards us. And even at a distance, I can tell the light walk and lithe build suggests it's Kelvan.

"Well, fellow losers – consoling each other?" he says, a bit mockingly, as he sits beside us. "Mind you, that Beaver's a good archer. But I still reckon the judging wasn't fair."

"Have you come to cheer us up? Because you're not doing a very good job of it so far," Sparrow remarks wryly.

"No, I've come about the tunics. If Rowan wasn't too busy practising with her bow and arrows earlier—"

"Of course I wasn't," I say indignantly. "Weaving's my job! I did the hawk signs before breakfast, as soon as the light was good enough."

"That's great. Because I thought I'd walk back with you and pick them up myself. But we need to go via the Northside camp first – if that's all right with you. My mother wants to meet you again."

"So she can pay me?"

"Well, that too. But mostly because she wants to congratulate you."

"Rowan, you were magnificent this afternoon." Kelvan's mother (I suppose she's Princess Something; he's not properly introduced us) takes my hands in hers. She also smiles at Kezzie, who's rubbing against her skirt, then gestures to me to sit with her on her couch. Kelvan and Kezzie sit beside us.

"Um – thank you, it's very kind of you to say so. But I don't think I'm as good an archer as Gerwas, generally. Today was lucky for me. The disguise helped."

"But that's just what I mean! The disguise! You were so bold and daring. I'd never have taken the notion to do such a thing at all at your age. As it is, you've fired a burning arrow to inspire all women – showed we can compete successfully with the men in more skills than they'll admit."

"I guess the men might not be so pleased."

"Oh, more than you think will be impressed with the craft and cunning of a nice-looking girl. There'll be many a toast to you in all the feasting halls tonight."

I'm a bit taken aback at such enthusiasm. I don't think my mother will share it either. Jelize did say "Well done" to me after the final results were announced. But I saw my mother stalking off without a backward glance. So it's nice to be appreciated. But I don't want to take undue credit either.

"Well – thanks. But it was my cousin Anyanda's idea in the first place. And she wasn't really thinking about men and women in general. She just didn't want Beaver Boy – Gei was – to win."

Kelvan's mother raises her eyebrows (thin and dark, like his). "Does your cousin hold this young Beaver in such dislike?"

Kelvan and I look at each other, and we can't help smiling. It's surprising how slow even sympathetic older folk can be when it comes to understanding young people.

"She likes him a lot, Mother," Kelvan explains. "Only she thought he wasn't paying her enough attention. I dare say they'll jump the bonfire before the end of the week."

His mother sighs. "I know you two must think I'm sadly old-fashioned. But I'm not sure all this letting young people roam around festivals finding their own partners in marriage is always for the best. My father would never have forced me to wed against my own inclinations. But Kelvan's father and I only met as many times as the fingers on one hand before the ceremony – only in company too. And look how happy we've been!"

"Yes, but—" I pause. She looks at me enquiringly, and I think Kelvan said she was a bit of a mind reader, so I might as well go ahead. "Didn't you know, though, when you first met that he was the man for you? Sort of soul calling to soul?"

She looks at me with interest. "Well, yes, Rowan, I believe I did. Although it took until the third meeting for him to realise."

"And did you see any pictures about him in your head, to tell you?" I ask eagerly.

"Oh, Rowan's a great one for mind pictures," Kelvan says with tolerant amusement. "She was telling me how she'd seen a vision of a shell closing, before those two characters I told you about set on us. But we got rid of them without any trouble."

I signal to his mother, with mind and eyes, to say 'please change the subject'. And I guess she understands, because she says, "Well, that's as may be. But in any case, Rowan's a young woman of talent. I've seen for myself that she's a dream of a weaver."

"My mother embroiders, you know," Kelvan says quite proudly. "These cushions are hers."

I've already seen Kelvan's mother has pillows for the day as well as night – and some for ornament rather than sitting on. These must be the cushions.

"The pictures on them are lovely. Are these mountains and waterfalls like the ones you have in the north?"

"They are indeed. And a hard job it was, having wools dyed just right for some of the colours I wanted."

"Oh yes! I sometimes find that's a problem, too. But this one – where you've got all the leaf-fall trees and the berries – that's wonderful!"

Kelvan's mother looks pleased. "Well, you can have it, Rowan."

"In payment for the Hawk signs on the tunics? But they were quite straightforward to do—"

"No, no. I've got some small jewels of Ezra ben Simeon's for that. You can keep them or trade with them. The cushion's just a gift. What we call a love-gift. Because you appreciate it so much."

"Well, I'll absolutely treasure it."

"Oh, you can always send me word if you want another at some time. And, on another subject, I'm hearing from my son that friends of ours seem to be your mother's brothers?"

"It sounds like that," I say cautiously. "Do they talk about us, then?"

"Only to mention a widowed sister, Raven, and her child, who live to the south-west among the Dragons."

"And you can't tell if there's more to it than that? Like, any information they're not telling you?"

She looks puzzled. "How would I be knowing that?"

"Um – well – Kelvan did say something about you being able to read minds."

"Oh, that's only in a small way, like most of us can. Except Kelvan, of course – his head's too full of music."

She and Kelvan smile at each other, and I realise they're the sort of family where parents and children really are fond of each other. (I also can't help wondering what it would be like to have a mother-by-marriage who's a mind reader. Possibly awkward at times!)

"Besides," she goes on, "It's not as if I'd try to find out a friend's secrets that way. Spying on them, that would be."

I can see her point, and I'm sure Jelize would agree with it. But it still feels a bit like a door shutting in my face.

"Well, Mother," Kelvan says, a bit impatiently, "I'm sure you and Rowan can talk mind reading – and wool weaving – another time. But she and I had best be off. I want those tunics for tonight's performance!"

So here I am, walking back to the West Camp. A lot of people are out, strolling and chatting to each other before getting ready for tonight's meal. And, I have to admit, most of them are stopping to stare at me. I don't know if this is because of the archery competition or because it's a bit unusual to see a young woman walking between a lynx and a prince, hugging a cushion.

"Kelvan?" I can't help asking. "Since your mother embroiders so beautifully, couldn't you have asked her for help with your costumes?"

Kelvan shakes his head. "It needs someone young to come up with the right ideas for designs. And it's your job – not hers."

(Oh well. I have been wondering if it was for the sake of seeing me again. I might have known that for Kelvan it's all about the music.)

"There's something else I was wanting to know…"

"I'm sure," Kelvan says. "I can see you're a great one for wanting to know, Rowan the Weaver."

"Well, when you were talking to the priest today – and before, with the Shell men – you saw they had respect for the Goddess. But I couldn't quite make out what you believe yourself."

"Oh, I believe in the three-in-one Goddess – the nine ways of wisdom – all the usual things," Kelvan says lightly. "Although I'm not sure why we think of the Goddess as all female. Why couldn't she be both sexes?"

"Or neither? Jelize thinks like that. That's why she says 'the Divine'."

"Yes… Would you like an apple, by the way?"

"Oh – yes please."

Kelvan holds it so I can eat as I carry on walking with the cushion. It's a bit strange to have him so close up, even though it's for a practical reason.

"I'm glad you think that way," I add.

Kelvan raises his eyebrows. "Why especially, Rowan?"

The answer seems obvious to me – it shows we think alike. But I realise I can't say so. "Oh – because it's a sensible way to look at things."

"Well, I do think there's a lot of superstition mixed up with what many people think of as religion."

"Yes, like Aunt Anya," I say with feeling. "Do you know, she threw her hairpins in the Big River, so we'd be safe going home if it rises. But they were only old rubbish ones. I mean, if the water spirits care about such things, wouldn't they know?"

"Talking of your aunt, isn't that her there now, outside your shelter? With Jelize and your mother?"

"Yes, and they don't look very happy!"

As we get nearer, I feel you could cut the air between them with a knife. Kezzie draws closer to me. Kelvan seems to ignore this feeling on purpose, and smiles around charmingly. "Madams Raven – Jelize – Anya! We were just speaking of you."

"And what were you saying?" my mother asks drily. "More to the point – what are you here for?"

"Oh, just to pick up our tunics."

"Look." Aunt Anya addresses the other women. "She's got princes fetching and carrying for her now!"

"I haven't!" I say indignantly. "I carried the cushion!"

My mother barely glances at it. I realise she'll be familiar with such things from her youth. "Cushions!" she says scathingly. "We've got more to think about than cushions, young woman. Wait till I tell you what's happened now!"

CHAPTER 9

After this outburst, my mother stands in the rays of the westering sun, her arms folded. Kelvan, Kezzie and I all look at her expectantly.

"This is a family matter, Prince Kelvan. Let Rowan fetch these tunics, then you can go."

Even the way she says 'Prince' sounds sarcastic. Kelvan's mouth quirks at the corners.

"Of course, Madam Raven," he says in the same sort of tone.

This time my mother almost smiles too. I can see she and Kelvan quite enjoy sparring with each other. The tunics are just to hand inside the shelter (though hidden under a very old rug, for safety).

"Rowan – I'll see you soon," Kelvan tells me. He kisses my hand – although I think this may be making some kind of a point to my mother – and waves an airy farewell all round before leaving with the tunics.

I put the cushion down on the grass. But carefully. My mother looks at it and sniffs scornfully.

"Is Kelvan's mother the one from the Green Isle?"

"Yes – but that picture's of the north—"

"I know the look of my homeland, thank you, Rowan.

I can remember Elcri's arrival. Of course, I met your father soon after, so I never got to know her. But she looked like the sort of person who'd produce work too pretty for practical use."

I should think this cushion can be both," Jelize says, "only, Rowan, there's something we need to tell you—"

"Yes, you've gone too far this time," my mother adds, with a sort of gloomy relish. And Aunt Anya chimes in with:

"We've had a summons for you. You're to see the High Priestess straight after breakfast tomorrow."

I gaze at their faces – Jelize's sympathetic, my aunt's gloating – my mother's a bit remote, as usual.

Kezzie moves closer to me.

"Why?"

"Well, I doubt it's to tell you what a good weaver you are," my mother says. "More likely to be about your little escapade this afternoon."

"But that's ridiculous! I mean, it was outside the temple. Nothing to do with sacred rituals, only the festival. The priest who was our head judge was quite nice about it, actually."

"Rowan's right," Jelize agrees. "It's hardly like committing a blasphemy. Or a crime. The worst that's likely to happen is that Rowan and her party – us – will be asked to leave the festival early."

"Well, I suppose that would be no bad thing. And, in fact, we could consider doing that anyway," my mother says, sounding more cheerful.

"If we leave of our own accord, it would suggest we think Rowan did something wrong. Which I don't," Jelize points out.

"And we are enjoying ourselves," Aunt Anya admits. (To be fair to her, she does work pretty hard most of the year.) "Shouldn't we wait to see what the High Priestess has to say first?"

"Yes, Rowan has to see her, now she's been asked," Jelize agrees.

As she speaks, Kezzie moves forward, tugging at her skirt and looking her in the eyes. (They can understand each other a bit, some of the time.) Jelize bends, then nods and straightens up and looks at me.

"Rowan – did anyone else help you with your disguise? Maybe with the whole plan?"

I can't lie to Jelize. And I reckon she's guessed the answer already. "Well, it was Anyanda's idea to start with," I begin to explain, rather sulkily.

As I say this, Anyanda herself strolls round from the other side of the shelter, as if she's come from the woodlands below. She looks a bit dazzled, and her hair's dishevelled. "Oh – good evening, everybody," she says, almost as if surprised to see us outside our own shelter.

We all try to explain about the summons at once, even Kezzie joining in with the odd howl. But my mother gestures to the rest of us to be silent while she tells the tale.

"So you see," my mother concludes, "as you were involved, Anyanda, I really think you should accompany Rowan to this meeting tomorrow."

Anyanda looks alarmed. Then her face clears. "Oh, no, I can't possibly, Aunt Raven. The stall will need me. Everyone will want to see Rowan, so trade will be brilliant."

She says it in quite a pious tone, and I can see she means it. Anyanda should live somewhere where they believe in little gods for everything. She would certainly worship at the shrine of a Trade Goddess. It's interesting, I think, how being at this festival is showing me people I've known for years in a clearer light…

"Don't worry, Raven," Jelize says rather wearily. "I'll go with Rowan."

"Thanks, Jelize."

My mother does sound appreciative. In a distant sort of way. And now we all seem to feel the need to focus on ordinary things, like changing before tonight's feast. Of course, there'll be no Kelvan and company, who'll be in another hall. But we have been promised some jugglers. And acrobats.

"Where have you been?" I mutter to Anyanda, as we wait outside so the older women have more room to get ready (or that's their excuse, so they can talk about us some more). "And don't sit on my cushion!"

Anyanda looks surprised. "Isn't it meant as a pillow for sitting on?"

(Maybe my mother has a point about it; but I still want to take care of my "love-gift".)

"Well – not when you've got dried mud and grass down your back."

Anyanda sits down on the hard-trodden grass with a bit of a flounce. "So what's this cushion thing, then? A *love token* Kelvan brought you?"

"No," I say crossly, "his mother gave it to me. Because I admired her skill with a needle. Kelvan did come for the tunics, but I carried the cushion myself." Kezzie gives me a sympathetic lick. "And," I add, "you still haven't said where you've been." (Something her mother would have been keen to know if this summons hadn't put it out of her head.)

Anyanda's eyes sparkle. "Oh, Rowan! Gerwas took me to a little woodland place where he could show me his arrow."

"But he'd already done that," I say, puzzled. "I'm surprised you didn't see me and Sparrow at the front of the crowd. We were cheering like anything, to be good losers."

"Rowan, you're such a baby at times," Anyanda scoffs. "I mean, his real arrow."

Remembering something Sparrow said, I gasp. "You don't mean you've mated already?" I ask, in a voice I can't stop sounding a bit startled.

"No, no. Not that. He knows he'll have to wait until the final feast night, when we can be married. He's been so sweet about it though – saying he can't wait to plant a baby in my belly."

(Anyanda's ideas of what's sweet must be very different from mine.)

"But do you want him to do that? I mean, your moon cycle's pretty regular. You might even start having a baby that very night!"

"Rowan, I know you don't like Gerwas—"

"I do! A lot more since the contest. He was so nice when he thought I—I mean Mab had won."

"Well, that's good. Only I know he's not the sort you'd fancy mating with. But if Kelvan said something like that to you, wouldn't you feel differently about it?"

"Umm – not really."

"Rowan – what do you actually feel about Kelvan?"

"If I tell you, will you swear by all the names of the Goddess not to breathe a word to anyone?"

"Of course – I swear by all her names," Anyanda says excitedly.

"All right. When he's near me – I feel as if my heart's singing."

"Oh, that's so funny. When he's a musician. And…?"

"Well, that's it, really." (Anyanda now looks disappointed.) "And I enjoy talking with him. But that doesn't mean I've been thinking of marriage, or mating. And certainly not about having babies. I'm not ready for anything like that yet. I've not done all the things I want to do with my own life first."

Anyanda looks at me with a bit of concern. "It's a natural thing when you're married. If you *couldn't* have children, that would be something to worry about. But if you're not keen, why not talk to Aunt Raven about it? She's always selling herbs to ward off babies back home."

"Yes, but she doesn't claim they always work. You know her views on that subject."

Anyanda does, and we chant in chorus, "The only sure way not to have a baby is not to mate at all."

"So you can see," I say, "why I wouldn't be keen to ask her, even if I needed to. But, to be honest, it does put me off the whole idea of mating. Because suppose she's right?" This reminds me of something else to do with marriage that cropped up this afternoon. "Oh, and it's a good thing everybody knows about you and Gerwas now. Because, from what Sparrow said, Crow was thinking of asking your parents if he could marry you."

Anyanda looks horrified. "Well, you'd better promise not to tell my mother. Because if she thought any Hawk, let alone of the richer, higher-born ones, wanted to wed me – you know she'd try to find a way to make me do it."

I nod in agreement. "Crow's a nice person, though. If you'd not met Gerwas, would you have considered him?"

Anyanda shakes her head emphatically, her dark curls flying about. "I'd never marry a man I couldn't fancy mating with," she says.

"Greetings, Rowan," Ezra says cheerfully as he joins me on my bench in the feasting hall. (We've not been told to sit in the same places as yesterday, but everyone seems to be doing it anyway, which has its good points – even Gerwas gives me a wave from the far end of the other long table, and I wave back, trying not to think about Anyanda's embarrassing remarks about arrows – although on the other hand, the argumentative man is still on Ezra's right.) "I hear we must congratulate you on your skill with an arrow."

That's nice. And I have to say, quite a lot of people are coming up to congratulate me, as if they think my almost-win reflects well on us Dragons – or, if they're Beavers, they're just being nice. My mother spears a lump of meat with her knife and ignores them.

"Well, I'm not as good as Gerwas, really," I say to be fair, as I pull a chunk of bread from one of the loaves placed along the table. "You weren't there?"

"No, but some of my men told me about it."

"You don't disapprove, though?"

"No. Should I?"

"Well, a lot of people seemed to think it was a good trick. Even the priest who was our head judge thought there wasn't any harm in it. Only now I've had a message about meeting the High Priestess tomorrow. My mother's not very happy about it."

"Natural concern for a daughter," Ezra says, adding reassuringly, "As you didn't break any temple worship rules, I don't see how anyone can mind too much."

"Any sensible person would see it like that. But my mother and aunts don't seem too happy about it – not even Jelize, who's usually very reasonable... Is it the sort of thing young women in your own country might do?"

"I can't imagine it," Ezra says candidly, "but that may be lack of opportunity. As well as women here having more freedom outside the home, the kind of clothes you wear as a protection against your damp climate must make disguises so much easier."

(Honestly! This obsession with the British climate! It's not always damp here, even if it is supposed to have got wetter in recent years.)

"It's interesting how customs vary between different countries, though," I muse (thinking at the back of my mind that I don't want to get tied down with a baby before I've seen some of them for myself). "I suppose some things must be the same everywhere – like having thirteen months in a year, because of the Moon. But think how we talk about the Goddess, while your people call Her a Him. Unless you're like Jelize, and just say 'the Divine'."

"An interesting woman, your Aunt Jelize. There's a group in Egypt who think like her, so I've heard. And there are some tales we all have in common – all the lands around the Middle Sea have legends of a huge flood many years ago."

"But we have that too! Only Britain was all right – it just got cut off from the Mainland," I say excitedly. "And there's the Green Isle – sailors who've been round it say you can see by its shape that once it must have been joined on to Britain. Maybe it just drifted away – but it could have all been the same flood, couldn't it – something caused the waters to rise."

"Maybe... My cousin Jacob would be interested in this conversation!"

"Would he? Is he interested in history, then?"

"More religious matters... He once wrestled with an angel."

"He *what*?"

"What you might call a good, or guardian, spirit. Your Aunt Jelize might say a messenger straight from the Divine."

"But I wouldn't have thought anyone could wrestle with them. I mean, they're *spirit* – so how can you?"

"Well, apparently Jacob insisted on it. And he's been lame ever since." Ezra can see my expression of doubt at this traveller's tale. "Oh, Jacob can be rather devious," he admits. "Gets it from his mother's side of the family." (I'm guessing Ezra's related through the father.) "But he's always seemed sincere in this. And nothing to be gained by telling a lie, either. Not that he needs any more lands, flocks, wives or sons."

"Umm – don't be surprised if my mother's a bit taken aback if you tell her about all this. She's pretty suspicious about anything supernatural. It's like the drugs priests take to help them with visions – the mushroom sort, or the very expensive imported poppy seed ones – ordinary folk sometimes take them too, especially the mushrooms, though we're not meant to. But my mother thinks the visions are all in people's imagination. Actually, she probably thinks that even when they've haven't taken drugs first."

Ezra gazes fondly down the table to where my mother's sitting by Jelize and Anyanda, chewing gloomily. "A wonderfully sceptical mind, Madam Raven has."

I nearly fall off my bench. Here's a man who expects me to believe his own cousin goes around fighting with spirits – well, all right, that was just the once – but you'd think he'd be throwing up his hands in horror and saying 'what a narrow-minded and dogmatic person'. Well, may the Goddess preserve me from being blind to someone's faults just because I've fallen in love with him!

The man on the far side of Ezra leans across and speaks to me. "Is it too much trouble to pass that flagon along? I've asked twice and you've taken no notice!"

"Here," I say rather coldly. "You could have asked Ezra to ask me, you know. You can tell he speaks British!"

He takes the mead, then says, as if to the sky, "The leaf-fall festival's not what it was. Too many forward young women and foreigners."

Ezra and I glance at each other.

"It's good to have somewhere to come and make friends from other places as well as trade together," I say.

The man waves his eating knife at me. "What d'you want to make friends with them for? Aren't your fellow countrymen good enough for you?"

I'm getting cross now. "I can be on good terms with

them as well! Aren't we all children of the Goddess? Or don't you believe that?"

"You're a fine one to talk, my girl! As if I couldn't hear you just now. All that blasphemy and heresy!"

"My daughter's asked you a fair question," a cool voice says behind my head. I realise my mother's stood up so she can look down at this man. "Never mind what other people believe. Do you think we're all equal in Her sight? Or not?"

Well, many cheers for my mother. This man actually looks a bit overawed. But that may be because she's tall and strongly built, and when her eyes are flashing and her arms are folded she looks quite scary. (Ezra, of course, is looking at her with even greater admiration than usual, if that's possible.)

"You needn't think you can cross-question me – just because you're some kind of Hawk."

My mother's origins must be pretty obvious, then. Though it may be her born-to-rule manner, not just general appearance.

"If you come up with ridiculous opinions, you're asking to get arrows shot at them. And I must say that this gentleman" —her voice and eyes warm a bit as she looks at Ezra— "has been a good friend to me and my daughter. What does it matter what country he comes from?"

Jelize starts clapping and, rather half-heartedly, Anyanda joins in.

"Huh! I still reckon the High Priestess would like to hear about the conversation he's just been having with your daughter."

"Well, Rowan has a meeting with her tomorrow. No doubt she can enlighten her then."

"I'm surprised you Hawks even bother to go through a priestess," the man says sourly. "Thought you'd just demand an audience directly with Herself." (I can't help finding this a bit funny. But then, I'm not a Hawk.) "Anyway, you can tell your precious daughter that festivals aren't just places to make friends. You can also make enemies!"

My mother rolls her eyes. "Oh, believe me," she says, "I try. I surely do try."

And now there's something to take our minds off all this: it turns out we're going to have a bit of a dance by moonlight outside the feast hall. As we drift out, I see Kelvan and friends have arrived. They must have come on from their performance in another hall to play for this.

Mart, Sparrow and Crow are getting ready to play. Of course, a drum really comes into its own at a time like this. Not so much a harp. And it looks as if Kelvan's not even planning to play, because he comes towards me and takes my hand, saying, "It's going to be a circle dance first. If we hold hands for it, we can stick together when we need to take a partner. That is, of course, if you'll do me the honour."

I'm glad he added that last bit. I don't want him to take me for granted. And the circle dance is fun and lively, as they usually are. Sparrow does call out a few instructions as he plays, to make sure everyone's doing the same thing. Most of the West Hall folk are here, although a few older ones are sitting on a bank to watch and clap – and the grumpy man seems to have totally disappeared.

Then it comes to a dance in couples, where we go up and down in lines. I can't help feeling a bit shy. Because it's hard to do this sort of dance without a lot of looking at your partner. I even trip at one point, even though my skirt's not overlong and I'm wearing good boots. Kelvan steadies me, and there's something warm and comforting about his clasp. I even start to wonder if he could give me good advice about my meeting with the High Priestess. But as soon as we've had the last dance – which Sparrow's told us about in advance – Kelvan just thanks me for being his partner, kisses my hand (that's the second time!) – and he's off to join the others. But at least a good finish to the evening should help me sleep well tonight!

CHAPTER 10

This breakfast's not bad – Bram, with help from Jelize and some of the men, has made a little fire, so we're getting some hot food. Which is good, because the morning's chilly – but fine and sunny, with a sparkle in the air. However, I'm really enjoying it, because knowing what lies ahead makes my hot oatmeal with honey a bit hard to swallow. Kezzie presses up against me, licking my hand.

"I'm sorry I can't go with you," she tells me in thought.

"I know. I don't expect you to," I say, knowing it would be too much of an ordeal for her to re-enter the temple. "I'll be fine with Jelize."

Funnily enough, I start to feel a bit better on the short walk towards the temple – the houses for the priesthood are built around it. Jelize and I haven't had much chance to talk on our own for a long while. I tell her about Kelvan's fight with the Shell men, and how they ended up being quite nice to me – it's her kind of story. When I finish, she nods.

"That bit about being treated with respect sounds like the key. It's what most of us want, after all."

"Kelvan's friend Mart reckoned I'd done a good thing. Though that might have been more on political grounds."

"It sounds as if he's heading straight for a place on the Council of the North," Jelize says rather drily.

I consider this, not sure if it's a compliment. "I should think he is, and he'd like that. More than Kelvan would, anyway – he seems to care more about his music than anything else."

"And you, Rowan. Since you've got to the festival, what do you want to do next with your life?"

"Well – it's been so exciting just being here, I've not really thought about that. Of course, I want to carry on being a weaver. And I'd like to travel with it – maybe Kezzie and I could go around British festivals like Kelvan and his friends are doing with their music – well, for the year they're allowed. But I'd still really like the chance of going to foreign places across the Shallow Sea. You couldn't try a bit of divination to tell me if I'll be able to do that?"

Jelize shakes her head. "It's 'can't and won't', Rowan. I believe it's best for people to work out for themselves how to weave the threads of their life into the best pattern. Although even then, a pattern which looks ugly, with untidy threads, may be beautiful on its upper side – the one we only see when we're in Spirit."

"Yes, that's all very well," I protest. "But I'd like to weave in some threads I like the look of now. So to speak."

"Well, the more reason for you to work that out for yourself," Jelize says cheerfully. "I won't always be around to answer your questions, especially if you do go travelling. And a lot of what we call fate is due to the sort of person you are. So if, for example, a determined young woman like you wants to visit foreign lands, she'll find a way."

"It's easier for a man, though," I grumble. "Like Sparrowhawk saying he wants to be a weather-teller who finds out how folk do it in other countries. His family and his local temple are going to back him to the hilt. Even though

I know he really just wants to go looking for fire-mountains.”

“Well, if your mother marries Ezra, that might open a smooth way for you. If you – and Kezzie – wanted to travel with them, I don’t see Ezra objecting.”

I stop in the path, even though we’re now nearly at the temple. “My mother! And Ezra ben Simeon!”

“Well, yes. Hadn’t you noticed his interest in her?”

“Of course! But I thought it was just – well, an old person’s fancy. I didn’t think they’d do anything about it.”

“Would you mind?”

“No! I’d be pleased. I *like* Ezra. Though I don’t know what he sees – and would my mother be interested?”

“Well, she seems to prefer him to any man back home. But there’s a barrier…”

“What sort of barrier? Is this more to do with my father?”

“We’ve no time to talk about it now, Rowan.” (Well, at least that’s an improvement on ‘it’s complicated’.) “But if you want, after this meeting I’ll try to explain.”

“Ah. Rowan.”

There’s a long pause while the High Priestess gazes at me. Her eyes are a light greenish-grey, with a kind of haze about them, as if she’s done a lot of staring into flames and water to see visions. They’re the same colour as Jelize’s, and I wonder for a stupid moment if all priestesses have the same shade of eyes. But I know better really – and actually the young priestess who gave us that talk on our first evening here had brown eyes. The overall feeling I get is one of power, and it’s tempting to look away, but I *won’t*. We’re in a small private room, with a little fire in a brazier. It seems very quiet in here.

“So. You’re Rowan Ravensdaughter. Or do you prefer to be known as Rowan the Weaver?”

I bow my head in a polite sort of way. "As you wish, your Reverence."

She smiles. In a tight way, as if it hurts her wrinkles. "Well, maybe we can settle for Rowan. Jelize, you may leave us now." They must see I look slightly alarmed at this, because she then adds, "Of course, you may wait for Rowan outside."

"I intend to," Jelize says coolly. She then curtseys and says, "Farewell, Mother." Which I know is how all priestesses address the highest one, so I suppose she still does it from habit. She gives me a long look, as if she's trying to tell me something; but I can't work out what. Then she goes out, shutting the door behind her.

The High Priestess gestures to a stool beside her chair. "Be seated, Rowan."

I do sit down, and she takes my chin in one hand, as if to study me further. I stare back, attempting to do the same.

"Well, Rowan," she says, letting me go, "you seem to be a bold and enterprising young woman. What would you think to becoming one of us?"

To say this takes me aback is to put it too mildly. "You mean – a priestess? I've never thought of such a thing in my life. So I don't see how I can have a calling for it. Besides, I don't have any special skills with prophecies, or far-seeing, or visions, or seeing spirits – not more than most people have. I really am simply a weaver."

"We can always use good weavers. I can see you're a very independent-minded young woman, like your aunt."

(I guess she means Jelize – maybe she's forgotten Jelize isn't my blood aunt – or, if High Priestesses can't forget such things, maybe she feels Jelize is an aunt to me in spirit.)

"You're not the sort to enter the service of the Goddess simply for security," she goes on, "or to escape a marriage your family are pushing upon you."

"I should think not!" I say indignantly. "I'm running towards something, although I'm not sure what – I'm hoping this week will help me find out. But, in any case, that would be an insult to the priesthood."

"Well, the Goddess can call us in different ways. I've known some young women who've entered Her service from such motives and made excellent priestesses."

"I appreciate being asked is a great honour – especially to someone like me, who's already a woman," I say earnestly. "But I believe in doing a job you feel called to because of a talent for it – and a real wish to do it."

"An interesting opinion. Of course, you've met young Prince Kelvan?"

I nod warily.

"So I gathered. Well, Rowan, you'll have to the end of this week to consider the offer. And is there anything you want to ask me?"

"Well, there is," I surprise myself by saying. "But it's not about becoming a priestess. It's just – if you don't normally see visions, but you want to find out about a particular thing that happened in the past – is there any way you can go about it?"

The High Priestess looks thoughtful. "There is," she says, "but it involves undergoing certain rituals which can be dangerous. So you would have to be sure you really wanted to know."

"Oh, I'm not," I say hastily. "It's probably something which doesn't really matter at all."

As I walk out into the leaf-fall sunlight and join Jelize, I'm feeling a bit dazzled in my head as well. This has been a lot to take in, and the High Priestess certainly is a powerful woman. Jelize looks at me sympathetically.

"Rowan – I think we need to eat as well as talk. Shall we see what we can buy for a before-noon little meal?"

I nod. "Only," I say, "let's make sure we buy it from a stall far away from mine. You know if Anyanda sees me she'll grab me at once, wanting to know what's happened."

One of the small, cheap bracelets Eleri gave me does fine for buying some bread, cheese, and berries made into small pies, with a useful wicker basket for it all. Jelize and I have circled round to the east side of the festival, where we're less likely to see anyone we know – although I do spot the Shell man who made his friend give me the magnificent present. He's going in a different direction, but he spots me too, and gives me a friendly wave.

"He looks like a nice young man," Jelize says as I wave back. "One of your Shell friends?"

"Yes – he's the one who was with the very drunk one, and made him thank me for my help the next day."

"He's quite good-looking, too."

"I suppose so," I say, thinking of his unruly brown hair and sparkling green eyes. "But I'm truly not here to look for a husband. And if I were..."

"If you were, Kelvan Windhawk would be your choice."

"Jelize, I just don't know. I mean, there's some kind of spark between us. When we first met, I got a picture in my head of two halves of a shell closing together – and I find him really interesting to talk to. But there are all sorts of things against it. For one, I don't really know what he feels about me. And he can seem quite ruthless. My Shell friend you saw just now told me Hawks aren't kind. Though Sparrow is. But maybe not so much the ones from really powerful families, like Kelvan and Mart. And Kelvan cares so much for his music – maybe more than for any woman. He certainly seems keener on it than the idea of becoming king."

"Well, maybe he should refuse any such offer. It's not

good to have a king who's ambitious for its own sake – if we have one at all – but one whose heart's not in it, and feels his calling lies in another direction, might be bad for Britain too."

"I agree! But he seems to be under a lot of pressure from his grandfather, the present king. Kelvan's his favourite, and apparently he's convinced Kelvan would make a good ruler. And then there's Firethorn…"

"Firethorn?"

"Oh – I've not said. She's some young woman from their tribe who lives near them. She and Kelvan have grown up together. Sparrowhawk reckons she'd like to marry a possible future king – even though she really prefers Mart."

"Again, a good reason for Prince Kelvan to refuse to be nominated as his grandfather's heir."

"It just makes me think how much easier it must be to marry within your tribe – or with one not too different and distant. And I have been brought up to distrust all Hawks, and stay as clear of them as possible – although when you think that was my mother's view, more than anyone's…"

"Let's eat," Jelize says firmly as we reach an open field. "We can talk more about your mother afterwards."

To my own surprise, I'm enjoying eating in the sun, sitting with Jelize. I'm starting to feel calmer, and more in touch with the person I was five days ago, before we set off for the festival. I've explained to her how the High Priestess had this strange idea of my joining the sisterhood, but was all right about it when I said I wasn't interested – and Jelize has agreed I've done the totally right thing.

"This tastes good," I say, licking the berry juice trickling down my chin. "So, Jelize…"

"Yes, I'll tell you what I know. It's not much, but maybe it'll be some help."

There's a short pause while we both stare at the stubbly field, which makes me think of winter garments woven from nubbly, thick-textured wool. Then Jelize begins.

"You know I was away at the school for girls intended for the priesthood when you were born. And, of course, when your father went to Spirit, when you were three. But I was back by the time you were six, and I started off living with Bram and family before I had a home of my own."

"Yes – I think I remember."

"Well, one day your mother came to see me. You and Anyanda were playing outside with Kezzie, and one of the boys who was too young at the time for the clay works was watching you. And Raven said she wanted to talk to me about something really important – divining the truth about an event that had taken place three years ago."

"My *mother* said that? But she's not someone who believes in that sort of thing, even."

"I think she was only asking because it was something really important to her. I was still young myself, so I didn't feel able to refuse when she was in some distress over it. And maybe I was flattered she'd turned to me – not just for any far-seeing powers I might possess, but because she trusted me to keep a secret. She said it was highly important I told no one else. Even when I knew what the answer was."

I draw a deep breath. "Goodness, what a thing to happen. But you were right to offer help. Did it not work? And that's why she's gone so unbelieving?"

"It did work – to a point," Jelize says slowly. "I came round to your home when you were in bed – and Uncle Ig elsewhere – so your mother and I could throw some rune stones."

"And what did she want to know?"

"Her actual question was whether or not your father's death was accidental."

"And…?"

"Well, Rowan – you have to remember these things are tricky – open to more than one interpretation—"

"But you're saying it wasn't. Aren't you?"

"Well, yes. And your mother didn't seem surprised."

"So – did you find out any more about what actually happened?"

Jelize shakes her head, her red-gold plaits glinting in the sunlight. "No. But you need to be careful how you search for the answer too. Because I had the impression your mother could guess the answer. But guessing is different from knowing. And – don't ask me why – she didn't want to know."

CHAPTER 11

As we turn back towards the stalls area, Jelize suggests, "If you like, Rowan, I'll go and tell Raven that there weren't any real problems with the Mother – and she was quite nice to you."

"Yes, and tell her about the priestess offer if you like. Although she'll probably just laugh."

"Well, that way you can get straight back to Anyanda. She must be getting pretty hungry right now."

I'm relieved, as well, that I don't have to see my mother again at this moment – as maybe Jelize realises. I'm still trying to take in this new information about her. It's very busy around the stalls, everyone out enjoying the bright day, whether they're buying anything or not. So I can't see Anyanda properly until I get really close. Kezzie's with her, and – to my surprise – Beaver Boy's sister is too. Although they don't seem to be having a friendly chat, to judge by the way they're standing – more as if they're squaring up to each other for a fight. Even Kezzie's concentrating on what's happening between them. So I'm almost on top of them without being noticed, when, to my horror, I hear Anyanda say:

"Well, your brother can marry this girl he's promised to back home, for all I care. Why would I be interested in Gerwas when I've had a marriage offer from a Hawk?"

"Oh – really?" The supercilious sister seems torn between wanting to believe Anyanda and doubt of what she thinks might be a made-up tale.

Anyanda spots me, and swings an arm wide towards me. "My cousin can tell you!" she exclaims. "She knows I've had an offer from Crow."

"Honestly, Anyanda, what are you playing at?" I mutter, after Beaver Boy's sister has turned on her heel and disappeared into the crowd. "And you've not really had an actual marriage offer from Crow. It was just Sparrow saying he wanted to make one."

"Well, there will be. I'm going for my noon meal – well, the one I should have had at noon, only you weren't on time – and then we're going to the North Camp to find Crow!"

"I honestly think you're making a big mistake," I tell Anyanda later that afternoon. I've had a pretty good time on my own – sales went quiet, but I've had a good chat to the bodyguard Ezra supplied for today. He's about twenty-five, from somewhere to the south of Egypt, from what I could make out. And although my Egyptian's not as good as I thought – maybe that's partly my British accent – we managed to find things out, by talk and by gestures, like his country having a blazing sun (well, I suppose it's the same sun, but it goes nearer Egypt) and the British weather making him shiver – he did buy a hooded cloak from me at this point. He's got a wife and children back home (I think) and he wears a ring on the third finger of his left hand, which I've heard married folk do in Egypt. He also managed to tell me Ezra's a good employer. Then – by saying "Ezra" and "Raven" and pointing to his ring – he seemed to ask me

if my mother and Ezra were going to get married. Which, as I've no idea, was a bit embarrassing; I had to pretend not to understand him at all.

Then some little children came up, wanting to know if his skin was black from berry dye; and he kindly let them rub it, once I'd explained, to prove it wasn't.

My mother came stalking back at this point, and frowned at us all laughing – she just doesn't seem to like any of our group drawing attention to themselves, as well as thinking my behaviour's a bit flighty for a single woman. But I'm getting to the point where I don't care what she thinks anymore.

And I've certainly got a lot of other things on my mind. Because Eleri drifted up when I was still at the stall, her retinue behind her. And when I asked her how Kelvan and his friends were (hoping somehow Crow had been summoned home before Anyanda could carry out her plan), she said that she thought the four of them were working on a new musical instrument.

"Kelvan's idea?" I asked.

"I think – his and Sparrow's," Eleri said. "Now there's a nice young man. Sparrow would make some young woman a good husband. If he weren't in love with my Kelvan."

"In love with – you mean he'd like to marry Kelvan the same way I – I mean, some girl – might?"

"Well, I may be wrong," Eleri said vaguely. "It may just be admiration. With my Kelvan being so handsome, and so princely in his manner – and so good at all he undertakes—"

"And because of that, so bossy and know-it-all…"

I was sure I'd not said those words aloud. But it must have come out as a noisy thought. Because Eleri looked at me, a bit amused, and said, "There's no need to shout, Rowan." Then she added, moving in a bit closer, "You have got a point, though, Rowan. You seem to be just the sort of

wife Kelvan could do with. Not someone who's interested in him for rank and money. But not someone who'll adore him and worship at his feet, either."

Goodness! I was quite taken aback that Eleri seemed to have such a high opinion of me – quite different from my mother's. But I wasn't sure how serious she was, because she then started talking about buying neck warmers for some servants back home, and asking a couple behind her which ones they thought the others would like. And once that was sorted out, she wandered away.

But a rather unnoticeable man, who had seemed to be part of her group, had hung behind. Then he came up to me. As he fingered some garments on the stall, he said – in quite a pleasant, low-key voice, as if making ordinary conversation (although Kezzie growled slightly) – "It's Rowan, isn't it? Now, try not to look startled at what I'm going to say next. Are you keen to serve your country?"

"I suppose so," I answered cautiously. "It would depend in which way."

"I'm asking because you've got a good trade to travel with – you're obviously a bright girl, not afraid to take risks – you showed that in the archery contest. You'd have a good chance, going around different festivals, to pick up any talk of rebellion against our rulers."

"The Hawk-led Council of the North! How would that help the whole of Britain?"

"Don't you agree it's the war bands that protect us from foreign invaders?"

"Well, I suppose so," I admitted. "But anyone might complain about them being too high-handed, or taking too many of our goods, without it being part of a plot. Less likely, really. I mean, if you were, you'd keep quiet about it."

The man smiled thinly, as if I'd passed some sort of test, which reminded me a bit of Mart.

"You see! It's that sort of understanding that makes a good intelligence gatherer."

(It seems like common sense to me, but you get a different view of things when you're never sat at the top table.)

"And of course," he added, "you'd be well rewarded, so you wouldn't need to worry about loss of regular income. And you'd still be following your usual trade. In fact, it would be essential."

"Well, I don't think I'm interested. Thank you."

The man frowned slightly, though still keeping his pleasant tone of voice. "We all know you've become a friend of young Prince Kelvan. But if you're thinking he might wed you – even if his mother likes you – it's only fair to mention—"

"I know," I said between gritted teeth, "there's someone called Firethorn he might marry. That's not why I'm refusing the offer." (Though if I hear her name mentioned once more today, I might just scream.) "I just don't want to go around spying on people – playing a false part. It's not for me."

"Ah well. You may change your mind. If so, you'll find me at the North Camp until the end of the week. And, while I'm here, I do like this tunic – although I'd prefer a more drab colour than scarlet. Maybe the russet one here..."

So it's no wonder that even as I'm telling Anyanda what a mistake I think she's making, my mind's still on other things. And Anyanda (who's not even bothered to ask me how my meeting with the High Priestess went) doesn't seem inclined to listen either.

"It's all very well," I say patiently, "for Beaver Boy's – Gerwas's – sister – to turn up with his apologies, saying he can't meet you because he's meant to marry some Beaver girl. But how do you know she was telling the truth, even?"

"Why shouldn't she be?"

"Well – because she doesn't want you to marry her brother?"

Anyanda opens her eyes wide. "Why on earth wouldn't she?"

"Maybe she thinks—" I'm *going* to say 'that you're too bossy and flirtatious'. But I think Kezzie senses this, and nips at me. So I change it to, "that it's better to marry within your tribe. I mean, some people are strange like that."

"So why didn't he turn up at noon, as we'd arranged?"

(All right, I can't answer that one.)

Anyanda goes on in a determined voice, "Anyway, maybe my mother's right. Maybe it's better to marry someone who can give you nice things. And – this is my own idea – maybe someone who's more in love with you than you are with him. So he can't make you miserable."

"But you don't have to marry anyone at all. Look at Jelize!"

"Yes, but she'd got used to the idea of not marrying, with priestess training. But if I come home from my *third* festival without getting married, everyone'll start to wonder what's wrong with me!"

"Not everyone. I wouldn't, for a start."

Anyanda half-turns as we're walking upwards towards the North Camp, and looks at me with a serious expression.

"Rowan, there was a girl in the next settlement to ours who wanted to live as a boy. And she did. And got recruited into one of the Hawk war bands – you know how they'll take suitable people from other tribes from time to time. She even rose to become a captain!"

"Good for her. But what's that got to do with us? Or Gerwas and Crow?"

"Well – you're so strange about marriage – it made me wonder…"

"Not for that reason! I do understand these things can

happen. Or" —thinking of my conversation with Eleri— "a man can fall in love with another man. And so on. But the point I'm trying to make is, a woman doesn't have to marry anyone, if it's not the right person for her."

"Well, I know you'll start holding Jelize up as an example again, saying she's made a good life on her own. But I reckon that's because she couldn't have the man she'd have liked. My father."

"I know Jelize and Bram get on well. But that's no reason to make up a romantic story about them!"

"It's not just me! I think it was really the reason Jelize moved out. Because I once heard my mother tell one of her friends, 'Of course I couldn't have someone under my roof who was too fond of my husband. Not that I had any reason to worry about Bram. He's the faithful type. Not like his father.' Of course, our grandparents were still with us then. But then my mother whispered – but I could still hear her – 'And certainly not like his brother, either.'"

My first thought is, How ridiculous – though like Aunt Anya – to think that, if those in Spirit can hear you at all, they won't know what you say if you say it quietly enough. As for the rest of it: "I'm not going to believe any of that just because you overheard your mother say it," I say in a determined way. "For a start, she might have made up all that about Jelize in her head. Because she didn't like having to share her house with another woman, so she decided to be mean to her. And I've never heard anyone else say those things about my father – or our grandfather."

"Well, they wouldn't say it to you—"

I override my cousin. "Besides, none of it makes any difference to my point about a woman being better off on her own, rather than with the wrong person. You don't have to join up the other half of your shell, you know!"

Anyanda grips my arm, her eyes blazing. "Oh, Rowan –

you're in love with one of the Shell men! Why didn't you say? Is it the one with the nice smile? I'll help you talk Aunt Raven round. And then we can both live in the north, and bring up our babies together!"

Honestly! It's nice she wants us to stay close cousins. But it's as if she's not heard a word I've been saying. Sometimes I wonder why I even bother.

When we reach the North Camp, I'm more struck than I was when escorted by Kelvan as to the different style it's got from the others. There's something a bit grim about it – more men who are plainly part of a war band – and I wonder now about some who look quite ordinary, after my talk at the stall with the intelligence-gathering organiser. We're also questioned by a guard as to what business we're here on – although once I say it's to find Prince Kelvan and his friends, it's like some magic talisman. Everyone turns very helpful, and points us towards the top side of the camp. Apparently we'll find them in some field beyond it.

I even pass the man from the stall, who raises an eyebrow and says, "Changed your mind?" I shake my head. Anyanda, Kezzie and I carry on.

"Changed your mind about *what*?" Anyanda asks.

I can't blame her for being curious over something like that. On the other hand, I realise I'm meant to keep quiet about that conversation. So it's probably best not to tell Anyanda, who could win gossip contests across the whole of Britain. Oddly, the one person I feel I could tell – because he'd keep it quiet, and maybe have some sensible views about it – is Kelvan.

And now the decision is taken out of my hands, because Anyanda, Kezzie and I suddenly hear a very strange sound – a kind of squealing shriek. We all look at each other, as if to say 'I've never heard anything like that before'. But it seems to be coming from a field where we can see the figures of the four men we're looking for standing around in a rough circle. So we all start running towards it.

CHAPTER 12

"We've been inventing a new musical instrument," Kelvan explains.

"We think," Mart adds cautiously.

I look at the object, which resembles a feetball but has pipes sticking out of it.

"It was you talking about silly games which put it into our heads," Sparrow explains. (Well, I guess, his and Kelvan's – I think they're the inventive ones.) "Mind you, Ezra ben Simeon went by, and he says he saw someone trying something similar in Egypt, but his didn't work very well."

"Yes," Crow says eagerly, looking at my cousin, "we thought, if we tried sticking pipes in, we could play them to make different sounds."

"Only, of course, with one person playing the instrument at a time," Kelvan carries on. "But maybe more than one playing, if we could make several instruments. I think myself it might be better than a harp to accompany troops going into battle."

"Why?" I ask curiously. "Because the sound would be so horrible it would frighten your enemies into running away?"

Sparrow and Crow laugh at this. Even Anyanda joins in, and Kezzie gives a kind of amused howl. So I realise I've got the wrong idea. But Mart looks quite interested.

"Rowan might have something there," he says thoughtfully. Kelvan looks at us all in a slightly disappointed way. I can tell he's got a sound in his head which this instrument should make, and he wishes the rest of us could hear it like he can. But he says quite cheerfully:

"Well, of course it needs to be developed. And maybe that's something for the future."

(Well, yes. But please the Goddess, not in my lifetime!)

"Of course, it would take a lot of skill and practice to play it properly," Kelvan adds, looking at it thoughtfully as it lies on the ground. "Besides, it's not very attractive-looking – not like a harp. It might look better with a bag over it…"

"In tribal colours," Sparrow chimes in. "A bag-pipe, not a bladder-pipe."

"Rowan – what a good thing you've turned up," Kelvan says. And I remember I want to talk to him about Anyanda – because if I can't put Crow off the marriage idea, maybe Kelvan can do something with him.

"All right. But if you want some cloth for this bag-pipe," I say firmly, "let's sit down and talk about it."

As I speak to Kelvan, Anyanda's already trying to sidle up to Crow, while Sparrow's Snapper – who's come out from behind a bush now the music's over – is making friends again with Kezzie. Mart's picking up the instrument to look at it. Kelvan looks a bit surprised at my words, but quite willing to go to one side of the field with me. Only at this point we have an interruption.

"In the name of the Goddess, what are you all doing here, making these appalling sounds? Surely you don't call that music?"

I realise at once that the tall girl walking elegantly across the rough grass, followed by a small gaggle of servants, must be Firethorn; and I can see what everyone meant about her hair, which is redder than mine, and thick, straight and heavy-looking. She's got pale skin (typical northerner) and her hair flops over a white fur cloak. I don't approve so much of fur – bad for my trade, and encourages people to kill other creatures just for that, not food. But I have to admit she looks magnificent in it. As she gets closer, I can see she's wearing a green necklace over her dark green dress, which matches the colour of her eyes.

"Kelvan," she breathes huskily, putting out both hands.

"Oh – Firethorn," he says offhandedly, taking her hands in a rather reluctant manner.

She kisses him on either cheek. Then she turns to Mart, saying "Mart" in just the same tone of voice, and performing just the same actions. Only Mart looks enthusiastic, and kisses her back. "Sparrow, Crow," she adds, flapping one hand towards them in a sort of disdainful acknowledgement of their presence. They just grin and roll their eyes at each other.

"Firethorn," Kelvan says firmly, "we have some new friends from the Dragon tribe for you to meet. This is Rowan the Weaver. And here's her cousin, Anyanda: her family make beakers, but for this week she's helping Rowan on her stall."

"Ah, tradespeople."

She doesn't look at us directly. But I address her anyway.

"Yes – it's wonderful to have a skill you can make your living with, and be independent. Although I realise there are some folk who don't do that, but could if they had to – like Kelvan's mother with her cushions. Do you have any particular skill?"

Anyanda looks at me open-mouthed. She does tend to be a bit deferential to the upper classes, like her mother. Sparrow and Crow look pleased, and slap each other's hands. Firethorn herself doesn't seem so much annoyed as puzzled. It's as if a clod of earth has spoken to her.

"Of course, I have a skill in managing a large household and entertaining important visitors at banquets," she says coldly. "Which will be useful to my husband when I'm married. You people who live in your little huts down in the south wouldn't understand."

"Rowan might understand more than you think," Kelvan says, sounding rather amused. "Her mother's one of us. From a good family, too."

"Your mother's a Hawk?"

(Firethorn's manner suddenly seems a bit less frosty. At least she's addressing me directly. What an appalling attitude!)

"Yes, but she doesn't bother with any of that now," I say firmly. "She just gets on with living in a small house. And working as a herbalist."

"And talking of trades," Kelvan cuts in, "Rowan came to see me on business. So if you'll excuse us, Firethorn? I'm sure Mart can show you our new musical instrument. Even if you won't appreciate it."

With that, he takes me by the arm and starts walking me to the west end of the field. Kezzie gambols beside us, so I think I'd better go – even though I can already see Anyanda sidling up to Crow, which I'm not happy about.

Kelvan pulls his legs up once he's sat down, so he can sit with his arms wrapped around his knees. He's one of those people who can look graceful even sitting on a piece of ground.

"I'm glad you got me out of that," he says as Kezzie and I join him. Then he goes on in a nice, if slightly teasing voice, "So what is it, Rowan the Weaver? Shoot straight ahead!"

I draw a long breath. "Well, it's my cousin," I say in a bit of a rush. "She's going to encourage Crow to ask her parents if he can marry her."

Kelvan looks a bit surprised (understandably). "That'll make Crow happy. But I thought she was interested in that Beaver – Gerwas. After all, she accepted his arrow."

"I know. But now it turns out he's promised to some girl from his own tribe. And his sister told Anyanda he thinks he'll have to stick to it."

Kelvan grins, and nods to where Crow and Anyanda have drawn aside to talk on the eastern edge of the field. "Lucky for Crow, then."

"But you don't understand! She's not in love with him. And she told me she doesn't want to mate with him."

(I'm surprised I'm not embarrassed to be talking about such things to a young man I've only known for a few days. But I always have found Kelvan very easy to talk to.)

He shrugs. "Well, your mother's a herbalist. Maybe she could give your cousin something to put her in a mating mood. Or if not – you know how there are always drugs floating around at festivals..."

"No, I don't, actually. This is my first festival. Remember?"

"Oh, yes. Well, you do know how the priesthood are allowed some substances to aid their trances and visions – all that sort of stuff? Of course, there's always someone along the supply chain who'll sell it to anyone if the price is right. Especially the poppy seeds, because they're expensive and come from abroad – not like the mushrooms you can pick up over here. There are some musicians who reckon it helps their performance. But I'm totally against it myself. I reckon you need to be in control of your mind to be in charge of your instrument. The others know I'll only play with them on that basis. Mart and Sparrow agree with me, anyway – I'm not so sure about Crow."

"But in any case," I say impatiently, "that's only a one-off performance that might be helped or harmed by someone using some drug. Marriage is meant to be for life! And would Crow want a girl who was really in love with someone else?"

"Well, he might. In the hopes he'd grow on her. You see, there's no denying some young women do seem to find male musicians attractive. I've seen that with me – with Mart – even with Sparrow. Although he never seems that interested back, except in a friendly way..."

(I thought Kelvan was good at observing people! He perhaps understands a bit more about Sparrow than his mother realises. I can also see why some young women would want to marry Sparrow, if they weren't too bothered about the mating side of things. He's funny, he's kind, and he knows what he wants to do with his life – which can be charming in itself. Mart, now – well, he and I can never be more than friends; but certainly some girls go for the grim, brooding type of man. And Kelvan himself – it may all be mixed up with the Prince thing, but it's obvious a lot of females would be attracted to him.)

"But not so much Crow?" I venture.

"No. Not because he's a drummer – even though we joke about it. It's – well, just being Crow. Anyway, you heard what my mother said about how many arranged marriages turn out well. Why shouldn't theirs – even if they're arranging it themselves?"

I'm disappointed. "So you wouldn't want to ask Crow not to marry Anyanda?"

Kelvan seems torn between amazement and laughter. "No, Rowan, I would not. And don't you think I've got enough troubles of my own, with Firethorn turning up to interrupt and bother me?"

(This doesn't sound as if Kelvan would want to wed Firethorn. But I suppose you can never tell with men.)

"I take it she's not keen on music?" I suggest.

"She doesn't like me being a musician. She thinks that should be left to men who can't have much choice of work – say, because they're blind – and that if you can be a warrior or a landowner, you should be. However much music you've got inside you."

"That sounds a bit bloodthirsty. The warrior part."

"It's not that exactly. But Firethorn's very keen on power. And she can't have those jobs directly – only through a husband."

"It seems wrong she can't. Except if she wants power for the wrong reasons. So maybe in her case it's a good thing."

"Of course, most of all, she'd like to have a husband who's a king."

I look at Kezzie. She looks back.

"Surely," I say, "you've got a simple solution. You don't want to be a king. So tell your grandfather you refuse to be named as his heir. Then if it's Mart she really likes" —we look to where she's drawn him away to the top north of the field, while Sparrow plays stick-throwing with Snapper— "she'd start leaving you in peace."

"Rowan – you've never met my grandfather, have you?"

"You know I haven't. He's left all the guarding of the south to his councils and war band captains since about the time I was born. Oh, and talking of that sort of thing, your mother came to my stall today. And one man in her group stayed behind. He asked me if I wanted to go round festivals as an intelligence gatherer for the Council."

Kelvan raises his eyebrows. "Well, that's quite a compliment. And you could be good at it. You're quick-witted, and you think outside the boundary field."

"I don't think it is! Asking me to spy on my fellow Britons!"

"Only for the country's good," Kelvan points out.

"What about the risk of accusing someone unfairly, just from an overheard conversation?"

"Well," Kelvan says, rather sarcastically, "wouldn't your mind-reading skills protect you from that?" He looks as if an idea's just struck him. "And talking of which…"

Kelvan unpins the heavy metal brooch holding his cloak together (I've noticed it before, and thought its rather old-fashioned look didn't seem like Kelvan's style) and hands it to me. "There you are! See what you can do with that!"

I stare at it in bewilderment. "How d'you mean? Use the pattern for a design?"

"Rowan – don't you ever think of anything but weaving? This was my grandfather's brooch. His giving it to me was meant to be some sort of honour. Try holding it for a bit, and see if it can give you a feel for the sort of man he is."

Kezzie growls a bit. But more in a 'be careful' than 'don't do it' way. I hold it doubtfully, passing it from one palm to the other. As I try to think about the previous owner, I can feel it warming up a bit. Then a picture comes into my head…

An elderly man is sitting by a window in a building which is actually made of stone – which means money behind it, and the need for defence. He's looking out in a brooding sort of way, but there's a large bronze mirror on a stand at his side. The room's quite bare, but it's easy for me to tell at a glance that the wall hangings and floor coverings (dark but rich colours, intricately woven) are of good quality; and the same for the man's clothes, although they're also dark, and sombre in style. A jewel in a gold surround glows amber at his throat. He starts to drum his fingers impatiently on the arm of his chair, as if he's waiting for people to arrive with news – maybe riding in? – who've not yet come.

As I look, a shadowy figure appears in the mirror to the side of his reflection. He notices it at once and twists round, eyes blazing. I hear a voice say in my head:

"Who dares to spy on me?"

Hastily, I drop the brooch in the grass, and use my hands to draw a grey mist down before me. No one's taught me to do this, and I've never felt called on to do it before – it just seemed to come when I needed it. And it seems to have worked. Because when I draw a shaky breath and look around, it's just me, Kezzie and Kelvan at the west end of a field on a hill, with a pale sun above us.

Kelvan looks at me curiously. "You can do it, can't you, Rowan? I'm never sure, with folk who claim to be far-seeing, whether they can really do it or not."

"Well, it wasn't very nice for me," I say indignantly, as Kezzie licks my hand reassuringly. "I see what you mean, though – if that was your grandfather. He is very scary! Although I still don't see why that means you have to become king – or marry Firethorn."

"Oh, I've no intention of marrying her," Kelvan says coolly. "That's not the real problem with my grandfather either."

I stare at him. "Oh. Other people seem to think you will."

"Probably because that's what she's told them. Well, they can think again. After all" —Kelvan suddenly leaps to his feet and pulls me up after him— "if I were to offer marriage to any woman at this festival, you should know, Rowan, that it would be you!"

CHAPTER 13

Kelvan and I stare at each other, his hand still gripping my wrist. For a moment, it feels as if there's only the two of us in the world.

"Well, have you finished this *business* talk?" a sarcastic voice cuts in. And I look round to see Firethorn and all the others have joined us at our end of the field.

Kelvan drops my arm. "Oh, I think we've said enough to be going on with," he replies in a light tone.

"Well," Crow says, grinning bashfully, "Anyanda's just told me something that makes me very happy. In the nature of – uh – personal business."

I see he's holding her hand and has a rather dazed expression, whereas she just looks smug and self-satisfied. He adds, "I can't believe my luck."

No, and so you shouldn't, I want to scream at him. I would try to do that in my head; but even if Crow could pick up a thought in the way Eleri or Jelize can, it wouldn't be possible to get it through while he's gazing at Anyanda in that besotted way. I think his friends share my doubts – because although they say "Well done" and thump him on the back, they're doing it in rather a half-hearted way. And now Firethorn joins in, saying in a graciously patronising manner, "Well, Crow, I'm sure this girl's parents will be delighted to hear a Hawk wants to wed her. But of course" —she looks first at Kelvan, then Mart— "festivals provide excellent opportunities for proposals."

"So they do," Kelvan agrees, "though not always from the people you'd expect."

That sounds as if it could be meant as an insult to Anyanda, for changing admirers, or Firethorn, for trying to run two in the same harness – or both. They certainly both look a bit unsure, but inclined to take offence at his words.

Then Firethorn shrugs it off in a haughty manner. It looks as if she's dismissed her servants earlier – maybe they've gone to plump up pillows and cushions for her comfort, or boil water over a fire so she can wash in some luxurious shelter. Anyway, she says to the musicians, "Well, boys. Aren't you going to escort me to my lodgings?"

And although they grimace at each other, that's what they get ready to do. Bag-pipes and all.

"You are a dark horse, Rowan," Anyanda exclaims as she, Kezzie and I go clambering down on our westward way. (We skirted round the North Camp on our way back, rather than tag along after Firethorn like more servants.) "I really thought Kelvan looked as if he was about to kiss you back there."

(Hey, guess what, cousin. So did I!)

"That Firethorn's so big-headed," she chatters on. "I don't think she likes Kelvan spending time alone with you. Which is a real cheek, when she's got that Mart. But maybe you think it's all right because you've got two admirers too."

"I have? Who are they, then?"

"Well, Kelvan, for one. And that Shell man you told me about…"

"I told *you*? Only in your dreams, Anyanda. And I must say, in fairness to that Firethorn as well as myself, neither of us have gone from accepting an arrow from one young man to then proposing to another on the very next day!"

"You're so *prim*, Rowan," Anyanda says despairingly. "The human race would die out if everyone was like you."

"Well, maybe that wouldn't be so bad. Leave the world to folk like Kezzie!"

Kezzie rubs up against me as we walk. I hear her voice in my head. "Some of you two-legs aren't too bad," she says.

As we get near our shelter, we bump into Aunt Anya, Jelize and my mother, who are about to leave it. They're carrying towels and spare clothes.

"We're going down to a pool – it's off a tributary of the River," Jelize explains. "The sun's warmed it so well, we're going to bathe there."

"Jelize says there are trees around it – but I've arranged for a couple of Bram's and my workers to keep guard too," Aunt Anya adds.

"I think you two girls had best join us," my mother tells me and Anyanda. "Without much spare water in the camp, I doubt you've been washing enough."

"And the mud can be good for our skins, can't it?" Anyanda asks eagerly. "Even if it's not as good as clay."

I agree it sounds like a nice idea. Only…

"I'd like to come. But I'd like a short rest in our shelter first. I've been on my feet for a long time! I'll join you afterwards."

"But Rowan – how will you find us?" my mother asks.

Jelize smiles at Kezzie. "Kezzie will pick up our scent. She'll show Rowan the way."

"Rowan! Hi, Rowan, wait for me!"

I can tell that's Gerwas's voice. And as Kezzie and I stop and turn on our downward spiral stroll to this pool, I can see it certainly is Gerwas. I'm rather surprised at his even wanting to speak to me. But, to be fair, maybe he's concerned for my cousin's well-being.

"Where's my Anyanda?" Gerwas demands. "She didn't turn up to meet me, and I've been looking for her everywhere."

For a moment my breath's taken away. But then, I always suspected there was something odd about that message.

"Well, considering your sister turned up at our stall, telling my cousin you weren't going to meet her because you were sticking by your promise to marry a young woman back home – what do you expect?"

Gerwas looks grim. He also suddenly looks more grown up, and I have another flash of seeing better why Anyanda likes him so much, quite apart from finding him attractive.

"She's gone too far this time! I know she brought me up after our parents died. And there is a girl she'd like me to marry – meek little thing who'd be under her thumb. But I never said I'd do anything of the kind. And I did trust her to pass on my message."

"So there really was one?"

(We've started walking again, as if by instinct. Which is good, or I'll never get to the pool today.)

"Yes, of course! But just to say something really important had come up, and I'd catch her after the noon lunch instead of before."

"Oh – I'm sorry…"

"Yes, your Dragons from the clay works suddenly called a feetball match with us Beavers. And" —Gerwas coughs modestly— "some of my tribal brothers wanted me to captain them."

I might have known. "So that was this very important thing? More vital than meeting the girl you want to marry?"

"Well, it was a pretty close-fought game. The Beavers only won just because someone scored before we stopped at noon."

"And I suppose that was you! Actually, I don't want to know. Thanks to that, Anyanda's almost got herself bound to marry someone else. That's why you couldn't see us earlier – we were up beyond the North Camp for her to organise it."

Gerwas frowns. Then he says gloomily, "I suppose it's that musician, Crow. I could see he was making sheep's eyes at her on First Feast Night. But she might have trusted me!"

I can't help seeing his point. "I did try to stop her," I explain. "But you don't know what Anyanda's mother's been like all her life, drumming into her head that she ought to marry for comfort and a powerful position. It's as if my aunt's been a bit disappointed in her own life, and she wants Anyanda to make that up for her. Although I don't know why she's like that. I mean, they've got the clay works. And my Uncle Bram's a really nice man, as well as being a village head – even if she doesn't appreciate him and tries to boss him around."

"I need to see Anyanda now and sort this out before someone rides off with her," Gerwas says with determination. "Where are you heading?"

"To join her and some other women for bathing. That's why I'm carrying this change of clothes, not to sell them. But you can't come in among naked women – and there'll be guards round the pool."

"Well, if you don't want me to try – *you'll* have to drag *her* out."

But as it turns out, Anyanda doesn't need much dragging. As soon as I've explained to her what's happened, she gives one shriek and she's out of the pool, pulling on a mix of fresh and used garments without bothering to dry herself. I'm still clothed, so I help her. The older women start to realise something unusual's happening, but they're laid flat soaking, with mud on their faces. So I call "Back in a moment" – meaning me and Kezzie – and go to the spot beyond the trees where Gerwas is waiting. They fall into each other's arms, and start kissing as if practising for a contest. So Kezzie and I leave them to it and return to the pool.

"Mmm, this is blissful," I tell Kezzie. The water's slow-moving, and I'm in a patch dappled by sunlight slipping between the trees. Some don't have many leaves left, and those that do make a dappled pattern on my arms and legs as I raise them out of the water. Kezzie, of course, isn't in the water – she's lying on the bank beside me, where I've managed to get into a little inlet of my own. I'm not a particular favourite with my mother or Aunt Anya at the moment – my mother because Anyanda's already told her we'd been up to the Hawk camp, and my aunt because I felt obliged to explain Gerwas wanted to see Anyanda, so she didn't think there was anything actually wrong with her daughter. Although I suppose, to my aunt, wanting to meet a Beaver when you could be with a Hawk is a sign of a serious problem.

"And really," I tell Kezzie – using my voice, as I tend to do when I'm also thinking things out for myself, "I don't mind if my mother and Aunt Anyanda don't want to talk to me at the moment. I need a rest from them!"

Kezzie leans over to give me a sympathetic lick on my face.

"And why are young men so difficult? Mind you, Sparrow's not too bad. And I expect Uncle Bram was always quite sensible. But look at Kelvan and Gerwas! You'd think Gerwas would put organising his marriage to Anyanda before a feetball game. And Kelvan to disarrange any ideas of him wedding that Firethorn before inventing a new musical instrument – even if it had been a good one!"

Kezzie gives me another lick.

"And," I add in a quieter tone, so neither my family nor a couple of other Beaver women in the pool can hear me, "I still don't really know where I stand with Kelvan myself. He told me if he was going to propose to anyone at the festival, it would be me. But that could mean he doesn't want to get married at all – not yet."

"Well, Rowan," Kezzie purrs, "would you say yes if he asked you?"

"Do you know," I say, rather surprised at myself, "I'm not sure."

As Kezzie and I amble along the winding uphill track back to our camp, I'm feeling nicely damp and relaxed. I'm also hoping we can now have a bit of peace, because I feel as if this has been like three days in one, and we're still only halfway through the festival week. But I know this hope is doomed as soon as I hear Anyanda calling to me in a loud hiss from the middle of a clump of still-leafy bushes.

"Rowan! Over here!"

Kezzie also tugs at my skirt in case I hadn't heard. So I go over.

Then, as I get to the bushes, I see Anyanda's face peering out from the middle, and an arm waving to me to hurry up. Then Gerwas's head pops up beside hers. As they're quite low down, I hope they've not been mating or something. But when Kezzie and I arrive at the clump they're hiding in, I can see they're fully clothed and looking anxious. Then, when I look to where Anyanda's pointing, I can see why. Because, on the men's side of the western camp, I can make out Crow by his tall, gangly figure. He's talking to Uncle Bram, who's tugging on his beard, but in a thoughtful rather than displeased manner.

"I think Crow's asking my father if I can jump the bonfire with him at the end of the festival," Anyanda mutters.

"Well, you can't blame him if he is. You more or less asked him to only this afternoon. Shouldn't you be going up there to stop him?"

"Well, I think it might be best if I tell my father I don't really want to marry Crow, then Gerwas sees him afterwards. More tactful. And Gerwas says it's fairer to Crow – it would be embarrassing for him if we turned up now."

"I can see all that," I say. And I can, although I'm not sure how much it's Anyanda and Gerwas thinking to interrupt Crow's proposal would make them look foolish. But even so… "I still think you should set matters straight now, before you find you're expected to jump the bonfire twice! Uncle Bram's always pretty reasonable. I'm sure if you explain it to him properly he'll understand."

I think I may be getting through to them; but then we see Aunt Anya marching up to Bram and Crow. It's a good thing they're all too absorbed in each other to look downhill, because Anyanda and Gerwas are now kneeling up to see what's happening next. Which is Aunt Anya giving a screech of delight that carries downwind, and throwing her arms round Crow.

"Oh no!" Anyanda cries, almost in tears.

Gerwas takes her hand reassuringly. "Don't worry," he says. "I'll catch your father on his own later. It'll be fine!"

Kezzie and I look at each other. We aren't so sure…

CHAPTER 14

"So, Rowan – I hear the meeting with your High Priestess was satisfactory," Ezra says as we get settled at our by-now-usual places in the feasting hall.

"It was – but how do you know?"

"I was talking to your mother earlier," Ezra says – but in rather a distracted way. I recall my mother will only know what Jelize has told her, and not about the offer to join the priesthood. Which actually makes two offers of a new trade – and ones, to be fair, where I could carry on weaving – that I've had today. (If you count my mother's sarcastic suggestion I should become a wool-gatherer instead of a wool-weaver, when I was slow changing for dinner, that makes three.) But Jelize is quite a tactful person, and I'm sure she'll have found a way to tell my mother just what she needs to know and no more.

I thank Ezra again for lending us a bodyguard, and what a good talk I'd managed to have with that nice black man who comes from some country south of the Middle Sea. Then we get involved in one of our discussions about different countries' customs and cultures. Although I can tell I'm a bit abstracted too, after all that's gone on, and wondering what will happen about Anyanda and Gerwas. Ezra asks me why the Dragons are different from other British tribes, who all seem to take their totem name from a real creature or an object in nature. I explain to him that dragons are real, just not in a way we can feel or hear with our ordinary senses. Then we get onto nature spirits; I tell him about Aunt Anya and her bent hairpins, which makes him laugh. Then he starts telling me about some desert spirits called djinns. I stop him there so he can explain to me what a desert is. So he tells me about them, and different ideas people have as to how they were formed or created.

This brings us onto the fruit and cheese stage of the meal, and he makes the general comment, "You're very interested in different places and people, aren't you, Rowan? And you'd like to travel. It seems a pity."

"Why?" I ask in surprise. "I mean, why shouldn't I have those interests?"

Ezra sighs. "Oh, they're fine in themselves. I was just thinking of the great opportunity you'd have had to travel with me if you became my daughter-by-marriage."

I glance at my mother. She's talking to Jelize and Anyanda. Nothing strange there. But her manner's livelier than normal (for her) and she's been avoiding looking at Ezra.

"So you – uh – don't think I'll have that chance?"

Ezra shakes his head. (He uses the same gesture for saying no as we do.) "I asked your mother to marry me this afternoon, when she was packing up her stall. I didn't see you and your cousin anywhere about."

"No, we were up beyond the North Camp – but I can tell you about that another time. So she said no?"

Ezra nods gloomily. "That's right."

"Oh, Ezra. I'm truly sorry. You've been such a good friend to us. I wish we could have gone with you. And not just on my own account. Although I'd have loved it." I bet Kezzie would have too – we might have got to Egypt, and they have creatures called cats that are a bit like little Kezzies, and everyone worships them – or at least treats them as close family friends. I almost hope Ezra will ask us to come anyway – but I guess, as well as not being the done thing, he'd be worried my mother would miss me. So I go on to say, "But because of my mother. I think it would have done her good."

"Yes – and I've enjoyed our talks, Rowan. I'd have really liked you to become my daughter."

"And you my father," I say warmly. Because although I'm used to doing without one, I'd be quite happy to take Ezra on – as long as he accepted the independent nature of British women. "But you needn't feel obliged to keep sending your men to guard us and our stall—"

"Oh, of course that can go on to the end of the festival," Ezra assures me. "After all, there are only two full days' trading before the final ceremonies and contests, aren't there? And then we all leave on the morning of your Sun's Day, if we haven't already?"

"Yes, that's right."

"What I will do," Ezra says, in a rather louder and more determined voice, "is to stop dining in the West Hall. My men have been moving around to different places to dine. They're quite keen to follow your Windhawk friends and their modern music – at least, the younger ones are..."

(Well, at least that's a tribute to Kelvan and company.)

"I think they might be playing here tomorrow evening," I feel it's my duty to explain.

"Well – maybe I'll just dine in the North Hall, with some of my old customers, like the Princess Eleri. But I told Madam Raven I was going to sit by you this one last time. To explain."

I put my right hand over Ezra's left one. "I can't say anything except thanks. And, again, that I'm sorry."

Ezra's eyes fill with tears. "The ridiculous thing is, Raven, that your mother actually seemed sorry. She didn't say 'I don't want to wed you'. What she did say was, 'I wish I could. But it's impossible.'"

Honestly! Why must my mother always be so mysterious about everything? I wonder for a moment if Ezra could have misunderstood her. But, apart from his British being pretty good, you'd be able to tell from someone's manner. And, let's face it, it's just the sort of thing I can imagine her saying.

Now someone's banging on the high table to make a couple of general announcements. And a priest is asking us to give thanks for what we've eaten. No entertainments tonight. So that's the signal to say us diners can walk about, break into little clumps and chat. I stay sitting, munching gloomily on a wizened apple. This festival's been a wonderful experience so far. But it does look as if I'll be headed straight back for my old home afterwards. When so much more could have come of it.

I do see Gerwas making for Bram and taking him aside. Gerwas is looking excited and making a lot of gestures, as if he's pleading his cause. Bram's tugging on his beard, as he usually does when he's considering something. But he looks quite sympathetic. So hopefully Anyanda will be off to join the Beavers. At least that won't be too far for visiting often. I'll miss her, despite her annoying comments – or, as Jelize would put it, comments I find annoying.

Ezra sighs. "Well, Rowan. It's been good knowing you. May Yahweh be with you – Aaron?"

Ezra half-turns as one of his older servants – a kind of foreman, I think – comes up to him. Aaron bends towards Ezra, and they start talking in Hebrew. I've realised Aaron's a fellow countryman of Ezra's, so that's not surprising. What is, is that they're looking at me as if I'm the subject of their conversation. Then Aaron straightens up and Ezra says to me, with a bit of a twinkle in his eye, "Apparently Prince Kelvan is outside and wishes to speak to you. If you're willing, Aaron can escort you."

Well, that's not made me feel any less surprised. Because I don't understand why Kelvan can't just walk into the hall – there's no rule I know of to say he can only do this to perform, even if he is from the North Camp. But, of course, this makes me want to find out what's going on. So I thank both the men and say I'll come – but with a doubtful glance towards my mother. Who hasn't looked in our direction once all evening.

"It's all right," Ezra says reassuringly. "If Raven wants to know where you've gone, she'll just have to speak to me, that's all."

Aaron leads me to a dip in the ground, where I can make out the blurred shape that must be Kelvan. It's easy to tell it's him anyway, because he's playing the harp softly. And, as usual, very well. Aaron gestures towards him, then turns enquiringly towards me. I guess he's wondering if he's meant to stay somewhere nearby. But I've always felt totally safe with Kelvan – which is interesting in itself. Besides which, there's no sign of Kezzie – and I'm sure she would have come back from hunting on the hills if she felt I needed her protection. So I make signs to Aaron to say 'that's very nice, you can go now'. Which he must understand, because he nods, makes me a kind of bow, and walks off in a different direction.

The weather's tuned crisp and cold – proper leaf-fall stuff. I shiver a bit and wrap my cloak round me more tightly. As I walk towards Kelvan, my boots crunch on the frosty grass, and stars from different constellations shine sharp and bright. Sounds of revelry from the feast halls are carrying from different directions on the still air. I find myself thinking: This is a moment I'll remember for the rest of this life and beyond.

However absorbed Kelvan is in his music, it doesn't stop him being alert to sights and sounds around him. Because before I get really close, he looks round. Then he slings his harp round his shoulder and leaps up.

"Rowan! You came!"

I'm about to say 'yes, but why the secrecy?' But he puts both hands on my arms this time, and pulls me towards him. Then we start kissing.

It's as if the ice and fires and stars outside are all blending in my head. We don't seem to be part of ordinary time, even. But at some point he lets me go, and we stand there looking at each other.

"Well, Rowan the Weaver," he says, "shall we sit down on my cloak?"

"Well, Kelvan the Harpist," I say, "I think we might."

Once we're sitting together, Kelvan puts a hand under my chin.

"Rowan – have you been kissed before?"

"Not properly. A couple of lads at home have tried. When they were a bit drunk, you know. But I wasn't keen, and I managed to push them off. What about you and young women?"

"Oh, I've kissed quite a few girls," Kelvan says airily. "But" —he looks at me intently— "it was never like this."

And then we kiss some more.

After a while, we just naturally seem to slide down so we're lying on his cloak. I'm not even thinking at all about Anyanda and our discussions on mating. So maybe it's a blessing that Kelvan's harp somehow slides towards the front and starts digging into me.

"Oww! That's not comfortable!"

"Oh, Rowan, I'm sorry." Kelvan raises his head. "What did I—?"

"Not you. Your *harp*. It's digging into me."

"Oh – right." Kelvan sits up and adjusts the harp. "There you are, my beauty… You know, Rowan, this shows you'll make a good musician's wife. You understand how important taking care of his instrument is."

I can't help thinking that, firstly, it was more myself I was thinking about; and, secondly, if I were Anyanda, I'd make some arrow-type joke about instruments. But by now I'm sitting up, snuggled into Kelvan's shoulder, with his arms round me. There's something nice and homely about this – like getting cosy by a hearth fire in winter – and I don't want to spoil it.

"Now that we know we get on well, kissing," Kelvan says in his now-customary decisive manner, "I'll tell Firethorn tomorrow that I've no intention of marrying her. *In front of witnesses*. Well, the rest of the Windhawks. And then," he finishes triumphantly, "I can feel free to speak to your uncle. *About us*."

He starts pulling me round for more kissing. But I'm a bit concerned about what he's said, however exciting the end part.

"Kelvan – you and Firethorn hadn't promised to marry each other, had you?"

"No, of course not. I've got more sense."

"So – why do you need to tell her you won't before other people?"

"To stop her pretending afterwards that it wasn't all clear between us. Save her making a fuss to our families."

"That sounds all right. But won't it be very upsetting for her, to do it that way? I mean, it may be just her pride that's hurt. But if her pride's a big part of her…"

I'm quite impressed with my point. It sounds almost like something Jelize might say. But it turns out Kelvan isn't.

"It'll be fine," he scoffs. "I'll just push her and Mart together. That should make them both happy."

There's something else niggling me. It's at the back of my mind, like a catching thread.

"And what you said about us getting on well, on the kissing side. Would you still have planned to marry me if we hadn't?"

"Well, I was pretty sure we would. So the question doesn't really arise. But that was part of my reason for seeing you on your own. After all, Rowan, you said yourself, about your cousin and Crow – if she didn't want to mate with him, it would make for difficulties in their marriage."

"Oh, of course! You won't know, but that's not going to happen now. Gerwas was only late meeting Anyanda because he was captaining a feetball team. His sister gave my cousin the wrong message."

Kelvan shrugs. "Some women are unreliable."

"Well, she wasn't just that – but what about Gerwas himself? I know he takes sports very seriously, even if they're not his trade. But you'd think he'd put his future wife first. Especially when they seem so keen to – Kelvan?"

"Not another question, Rowan the Weaver?"

"Just – well, I know you've kissed other girls. But have you – you know – actually mated with anyone?"

Kelvan appears to be searching his memory.

"Oh, no," he says lightly. "I've not done *that* yet."

CHAPTER 15

Honestly, I can't believe what Kelvan has just said. Or, rather, the way he's said it. In one way, I'm relieved – I wouldn't want him to be too much more experienced in these matters than I am. On the other hand, I'm a bit taken aback by the way he doesn't sound as if it's even important. It's as if he's got a list in his head of things he means to do some time – probably one where 'Mating and Marriage' comes way down below 'Making a New Musical Instrument'.

However, he does then continue more seriously, "I did have a talk with my father about that sort of thing once. And he said he'd waited until he and my mother were married. Because everyone expected my mother not to have gone with any other man – especially with her being a princess. And he thought it should be the same for both of them."

My eyes open wide with surprise. "That's great! I don't know many men who think like that."

"Well, I think my father was a bit shy in his youth, which probably helped. With women. And in general. Growing up with my grandfather, you can understand that. Of course, he – the king – didn't think much of my uncle for putting stargazing before having children. As he saw it. My impression was, my uncle and my aunt were happy enough. After all, there are plenty of reasons why a woman can't conceive, whatever prayers or potions you try… Come to that, Grandfather's a bit scornful of my parents for only having two surviving sons – the younger ones are all girls, you know."

"Well, I do now. So you've got sisters?"

"Yes, but much younger. Of course, if my grandfather and the Council believed in the old ways – the kingship going to a sister's son – it would be different again."

"And wrong! I mean, I don't see why we can't have a queen in charge instead of a king. I know people would say 'what about leading the country in battle, that's easier for a man' – but a ruler can plan battle tactics behind the scenes – like your grandfather does, now he's old. But if we do have kings at all, surely the safest way is for at least some of us to have some choice in who they are – not to get a really bad one, you know."

"Oh, I agree. With the principle. It's just that if the country had kept to that tradition, Mart would be next in line for the kingship. Our fathers were cousins, you see. And his grandmother was my father's sister."

"I didn't know any of that," I say rather indignantly, feeling I should have been told. It explains a lot.

"There hasn't been much time for me to draw you a picture of my family tree in the earth," Kelvan points out. "Anyway, all of us from the north are some kind of cousin to each other if you trace it back…me, Mart, Crow, Sparrow, Firethorn…"

"I suppose it can be like that in a tribe. Only, where I live, some Dragons descend from folk who came across the Shallow Sea, and married with people already here. Especially where we are – not that far west. So it's different for me."

"Yes – although you might be distantly related to some of us. Through the mother, again."

"Well, very distant, I should think," I say doubtfully, "if my mother's brothers are no more than your family friends." (And that's not something I talked to my mother about, in case her knowing Kelvan knows them makes her start on again about going home early.) "But it must be hard for Mart – knowing if things had been different… And him in love with that Firethorn, the Goddess knows why, and knowing it would please her to marry a king… Do you always feel *safe* with him around?"

Kelvan laughs – rather mockingly. "You're starting to sound like a Hawk, Rowan." (I don't much like the sound of that.) "And yes, I do. Completely safe. Mart's extremely loyal. My father became like his, after his own father was killed in a sea battle against raiders from a country to the north-east of Britain." (Poor Mart. Maybe he's got things to look grim about.) "And you have to think, Rowan – all the times Mart and I have fought back to back – in warrior training, but also in real skirmishes – as well as being travel companions now. Don't you think if he'd wanted, he could have contrived an 'accident' a hundred times over? In warfare all it would take is one stumble to let an attacker in over your guard. Only, as well as knowing it would be wrong, Mart is like another brother to me. And I really don't think he'd actually want to."

"That's good."

"Yes. He wasn't even happy about our encounter with the Shell men. He doesn't really think I should go about on my own without him and the others around to guard me."

"Well, I wouldn't have wanted them here tonight!"

"No. Nor me," Kelvan says, grinning.

"But it's still nice of him – and trying not to mind about this king thing."

"Yes, but I mind for him," Kelvan says vigorously. "He'd make a far better ruler than I would – at least he's interested, as well as having the right sort of skills. But my grandfather has it in his head that Mart would be better as the Council member who's also my right-hand man."

"Well, I can see that working, too. But it's not about what either of you want."

"Well, my grandfather does care about Britain, and thinks that's the best way to protect the whole country. It's certainly not to please me – after all, he already knows I'm not keen to be named as his successor. Although that is why he agreed it was only fair I could at least have a year travelling with my music. You see, I'm his favourite." (So why can't he leave you alone, then?) "My elder brother – he's happy as a land manager, and Grandfather's happy to leave him like that. It's also why he doesn't care if I marry Firethorn or not. It was more that he thought, if I cared for her, she could talk me into being named as his successor without any arguments. Otherwise – I dare say he thinks I could make a more advantageous match."

"Like your father did with your mother! But in that case, what will he think of me?"

Kelvan shrugs. "If your uncle and my mother agree, we'll be married by the end of the week. Of course, I'll send my grandfather a message – give him time to get used to the idea before we meet again. And I know you'll be happy to travel with me and the other musicians."

"What about them, though? What will they think of you taking a wife along – even if I'm busy with my own trade?"

"Oh, they all like you, Rowan. Sparrow and Crow have told me how much they prefer you to Firethorn. And she wouldn't fit in with a travelling lifestyle either – not unless she was going from one stronghold to another, with about a hundred servants to wait on her."

"But what about your pact – the not-marrying one?"

"That! You've already seen how the others would break it in the time it takes to shoot a single arrow. Crow – poor man – if he could wed your cousin. And Mart, Firethorn. Which I'm hoping now that he will. And then we can all work together to influence my grandfather over the succession."

(That could work. And the man I saw when holding the brooch may have been old. But he didn't look ready to pass to Spirit any time soon.)

"And what about Sparrow?"

"Well – if he could meet a man who'd make a good life-companion for him – and can understand his crazy idea of going to find fire-mountains – the same applies." (So Kelvan does realise.) "I think the world of Sparrow myself. But not in that way. I suppose it just comes naturally to me to fall in love with girls. Although, of course, not seriously until now."

"I'm glad you've said that," I admit. "You were making it sound a bit as if I was just going to be a more useful sort of musician's wife than Firethorn. And this is all so new to me. I'd quite planned to live as a single woman, like Jelize. But, of course, I'd not met you."

"The other half of the shell?" (Well done, Kelvan. He does remember. And understand.) "And anyway, Rowan, don't you think that you know when someone's right for you – not just from kissing, but if they like some of the same things as you? And have some of the same aims in life? For example, I know we'll have a marvellous time on the road together!"

"For a year," I point out. "What happens after that?"

"Well – I suppose then we *will* have to go home."

At this point, Kezzie arrives. And I realise everything has gone quiet and cold around us. So – after hugging Kezzie to me, and enjoying the warmth of her fur – I agree with Kelvan that we'd both better head for our camps. I'm now starting to worry about Kelvan's general safety, going about as freely as he does, after our talk. Of course, to our Shell friends he was just an annoying Hawk musician. He made it plain at our first meeting that he doesn't use the title 'Prince' – and even if he did, princes aren't that uncommon, even if they are more usual in the Green Isle, his mother's homeland. But is it commonly known, at least among Hawks, about his grandfather wanting him named as heir to the kingdom? And if so, might he be at risk of – say – capture for ransom? I'm not too happy about this – or how it might affect my own freedom in future. But I see him catch up with a few Hawk stragglers – one of whom looks stocky and square-built, which I guess is Mart. So at least we'll both have company on the way back.

It's only on the way back with Kezzie – I tell her what's happened, but I feel she knows a lot of it already – that Kelvan's answer to my last question comes back to me. And I think, Yes, but it's not *my* home.

CHAPTER 16

The candles in the chapel, which have been burning clear and straight, are now being allowed to gutter out, as those of us who've attended a dawn service get ready to leave. We haven't gone to one before during this week; but Jelize said as it was a women-only service, and one being led by the High Priestess herself, we should all make an effort to go. And Jelize can be quite persuasive when she likes, because Anyanda, my mother, my Aunt Anya and I all trailed along after her.

It's turned damp but stayed cold. Attending an early-morning service is meant to be a good start to a day. But I've only been able to think how uncomfortable everything is. Older people coughing off-puttingly during the service, and even the lurid streaks of yellow light in the clouds: none of it's making me feel holy – just keen to get back to camp and help cook some breakfast.

But I can see I'm not going to be allowed that – or not straight away. Because, as everyone's filing out behind the priestesses, Aunt Anya gestures to me, my mother, Jelize and Anyanda to remain behind. She says, in what I can tell she thinks is a thrilling and mysterious tone, "Women of our family! I have had most exciting news from my husband last night, which I feel I can no longer keep to myself. Anyanda, my daughter – we have received a most favourable offer of marriage for you."

Anyanda turns to me in delight, and hugs me. "You see, Rowan! I knew my father would agree when Gerwas explained everything to him. Gerwas told me last night they'd had a really good talk. I wanted to tell you then, only you were back so late I'd fallen asleep."

Aunt Anya gives the impression of rearing herself up, like a snake about to strike. "Gerwas!" she hisses. "I've already told Bram what sort of answer he can give Gerwas. I was talking about one of the Windhawks – Crow."

Anyanda stands very straight, her dark eyes blazing. "What did you do that for, Mother?" she demands. "I've no intention of marrying Crow. Gerwas is the man for me!"

My aunt strikes Anyanda across the cheek by way of an answer. We all gasp. My aunt could be heavy-handed with her boys when they were growing up. But Anyanda's always been like her own little princess, to be petted and indulged. Anyanda herself, although she puts a hand to her face, seems more bewildered than hurt. Jelize moves to put an arm around her, while my mother digs into the bag she always carries with remedies for small injuries, digs out a little pot of salve and presses it into Anyanda's hand. That shows whose side they're on. Or maybe that's going too far – I don't really know what they think of Anyanda's marriage proposals – but they plainly disagree with the way Aunt Anya's handling the situation.

As for her, she now glares at me and my mother, and says, as if spitting out the words, "We've never had this kind of trouble at festivals we've taken Anyanda to before. This must be what comes of agreeing to bring a couple of free thinkers with us, and letting her help on one of their stalls!"

(I didn't know before that folk called me and my mother 'free thinkers'. I'm not even sure what it means. But it sounds to me like a good thing to be.)

"Really, Anya," Jelize says in a cool tone, her arm still round Anyanda, "I don't see how Raven or Rowan's beliefs can have any bearing on this situation. It simply happens that the first time Anyanda's aunt and cousin have accompanied you is also the same time two young men have fallen in love with her."

"That's true, Aunt Jelize," Anyanda says gratefully. "But the other thing is – I don't believe Crow's really in love with me, any more than I am with him. It's just that with his friends – the other musicians – Kelvan's got Rowan" —I see my mother stiffen— "Mart's got Firethorn – Sparrow's got one or two girls interested in him back home, even if the others say he's not so keen on them. So of course Crow wants a woman too – and because I'm pretty, and lively, he thought I'd do. Then I had a quarrel with Gerwas, which was all his sister's fault. It's true I did give Crow some encouragement, before I found out that Gerwas's sister had lied to me. And I can see I treated Crow badly – I will apologise to him when I get the chance. But it doesn't make any difference about me and Gerwas. We're right for each other. We're what Rowan, in her fancy way, would call two halves of the same shell."

I think this is a pretty good speech of Anyanda's. To be honest, I'm quite impressed: that she's had all these sensible thoughts about her and Crow, and that she's been prepared to tell us. But Aunt Anya looks all the more cross.

"You ungrateful girl! After all we've done for you, you throw away a chance to marry into a rich, well-connected family – and to a man who's not just an ordinary Hawk, but a close friend of someone who's going to be our future king."

"We don't know that at all. About Kelvan," I say determinedly. "The Council's not chosen yet."

Aunt Anya looks at me as if I'm an insect. Brushing my objections aside, she goes on, "You young people – you think marriage is all about four bare legs in a bed. But there's a lot more to be thought of in the long run than just mating. After all, I wouldn't ever have said Bram was the most exciting man a girl could meet. But what I could see was he had good artistic skills he used in the family's beaker works – he was good at listening to two sides of a dispute, which would help get him chosen as a village headsman – and he was a decent, honest, reliable person. One I could trust not to come home drunk, except on special occasions, and one who wouldn't chase after other women. And in return I've been a good wife to him. Borne him children – shared in running the clay works and the beaker factory – and always made sure there were good meals on the table."

"But you're not always very nice to him!" I can't help protesting. "My Uncle Bram's a lovely person. He deserves better than that!"

Now Aunt Anya looks really angry. She takes a step towards me, and I wonder if she's going to try hitting me too. I'm touched that my mother's taken a couple of paces towards me, as if to come between us.

"You're just a romantic, Rowan!" Aunt Anya says – as if being a romantic is like being a slug. (Not that slugs don't have their place in nature too, of course.) "Look where marrying for love got your mother! As if I hadn't turned Arvan down first. Because I could see that, despite all his good looks and charm, and sweet words and sweet songs, and, yes, having a great talent for his trade, he was a fickle, unreliable person who could never make a woman happy."

Well, what a shock! I feel as if I'm standing near one of Sparrow's fire-mountains and it's suddenly erupted. Everyone looks shaken. Even Aunt Anya looks a bit abashed, as if she's gone too far. Because, of course, Arvan was my father.

"Anya – you're letting your temper rule your tongue," Jelize says. "Rowan – are you all right?"

I'm not sure. My legs feel a bit unsteady. It's not that I'm totally surprised if my father did ask Anya to marry him, before he'd even met my mother. I guess Aunt Anya looked like Anyanda does now when she was young. And maybe she was merry and cheerful then, too. I can't say marrying for practical reasons seems to have done her character much good. I think it's more all the feelings swirling around me, like angry storm clouds coming from at least three people in the room, which I find upsetting.

Jelize moves to take a small, stoppered beaker from my mother – her remedies are certainly getting well used today! The beaker, when Jelize has pulled out the plug and given it to me, is a herbal potion I'm meant to sniff. It's got a pretty sharp aroma; but I have to say that a couple of deep breaths from it seem to settle me down. It also seems to clear my thoughts. Because I can see both my aunt and cousin are women who could only be happy with a marriage to a forceful man – not someone they can push about. And at least Anyanda's had the sense to see it in time. Which makes it all the more important she should marry Gerwas, not Crow.

"I'm sorry, Raven." Aunt Anya actually apologises. "But I am thinking of this girl of yours, with her high-flown notions. I expect she thinks Prince Kelvan will marry her. If you're not careful, she'll end up with a baby and no husband."

"Well, I'm sure we'd stand by her if that were the case. You shouldn't be so ready to condemn women who have a child without a husband," Jelize says – sounding upset, which isn't like her. "But I don't think it's come to that – has it, Rowan?"

I shake my head. "And in any case, Aunt Anya," I point out, "Kelvan's intentions are completely honourable." (I doubt she'll like that – she wouldn't want me and not her daughter to marry a prince. Unless she could see ways to hang on to us for things she wants – which would be awful.)

"You sound very sure about that, young woman," Aunt Anya says suspiciously. "How do you know?"

"Well" —I wonder if I'm being rash saying this, but know I can't help it— "He said after he'd – um – sorted something out this morning" —I can't explain about Firethorn, or they'd think Kelvan *was* just like my father— "he's going to talk to his mother and Uncle Bram about our wedding."

"Oh, Rowan," Anyanda exclaims, "that's great news!"

"No, it's not," my mother says curtly. "Rowan – we need to talk alone."

"And Anyanda and I must talk to her father," Aunt Anya says.

Anyanda pulls a face at me as if to say 'do something'. Because we've never known her father able to stand up to her mother in an argument. And I nod back. I'll certainly do what I can. Although I'm not sure who to go to about it all first – Gerwas or the musicians. And at the moment I can't do either, because my mother has seized me by the arm and is practically dragging me uphill – as if even the doorway of an empty chapel isn't private enough for what she's going to say. I try to mutter something about talking after breakfast. But she quells me with one look from her frosty grey eyes.

When we reach the summit of a hill slope, she sits down and gestures to me to join her. Then she stares into the middle distance – to the westerly hills at the far side of the camp, shrouded in leaf-fall colours, russet and gold under a grey-mist sky.

"I had hoped," she says slowly, "that I'd never need to have this talk with you, Rowan. But I can see I have to explain why I'm not happy for you to associate with Hawks.

It all goes back to your father..." (A lot of things around here seem to!) There's a pause. Then my mother says in a small, hard voice – still without looking at me – "You see, Rowan – I think I killed him."

CHAPTER 17

"What do you mean," I demand, "you *think* you killed him? Did you leave some of your herbs lying around – or distilled – like the one that's good for your heart in small doses, but stops it if you have too much? But why would he have taken them…?" I gaze at my mother in horror. "You didn't put them in his mead or something on purpose, did you?"

My mother sighs. "No, Rowan. Of course not."

"Well, what did happen then?" I ask, starting to get impatient. "Wasn't it true that he fell off some planking on a henge he was restoring?"

"Oh yes. That's true enough."

"Well, how *could* that have been anything to do with you? Unless you packed him some mushrooms to eat – and they were the sort that make folk think they can fly…"

"Rowan – stop imagining it was anything I gave Arvan. Or to do with herbalism, which I wasn't trained in at the time. It was something I said to my brothers…"

This time I give my mother the chance to collect her thoughts. Then she continues.

"My brothers were combining paying a family visit with helping Arvan on some restoration work. It was too big a job for one man. Of course, he could have used local builders –

and did, for some odd jobs. But my brothers were especially skilled in their field – like Arvan – and understood about the design side, and how to instruct others..."

She pauses again, staring – now rather sadly – at the far landscape. I try to think of a remark which will encourage her to go on. Or a question. "Was that how you got to know my father in the first place? Or did you meet at a festival?"

"Well, they made friends with Arvan at a festival in our part of the country. They were all still quite young men, although my brothers were already married with children. Of course, designing and building on a large scale was something they had in common" —my mother says this with a touch of pride in her voice— "so I got to know Arvan through them. He was so different from all the men I knew back home – always laughing, always prepared to dance and sing... We fell in love instantly." She has a dreamy moment, then adds briskly, "Which is why I don't want you doing the same."

"But Kelvan's not really like my father – even if he sings! He's got very serious views," I protest. (And I'm not the same sort of person as you, either.)

My mother brushes my remark away with a dismissive gesture of her hand. "So we jumped the bonfire," she says, "and he took me back to his homeland. Of course, he already had a good name there for his work, as my brothers had in the north, so I expected no less. And we were happy enough to start with, although I found I missed my own place more than I expected. Of course, we had a lot to do with Bram and Anya, as Arvan's brother and sister-in-law. Bram was a delightful man, but I found Anya trying from the start." (Doesn't surprise me.) "She seemed to think I put on airs just because I was a Hawk." (No, you did that just because you're you.) "Of course, she'd got used to seeing herself as Queen Bee of the village, through her marriage, and she wasn't too keen on a younger woman who didn't defer to her coming to live there. Then you were born – only about ten months after my marriage… Your father was delighted."

My mother's certainly taking her time over this tale. If she was a travelling ballad-singer, her audience would be shouting at her to get to the point of her story. But it's about my family, so I'm interested.

"Didn't that draw you closer together, though? I mean, having a baby you both wanted?" I now look at my mother with a bit of alarm. "Or do you mean you didn't?"

"You were wanted, Rowan – never think otherwise," my mother says swiftly. "But although this was before your father's mother went to Spirit – and you'll recall she was a lovely person – I did miss having my own family nearby. Then I started to realise that, in some ways, Arvan could be like a child himself. A charming, delightful one. But he wasn't someone who was willing to shoulder responsibilities outside his own work. If you had any sickness, he was always 'Oh, it'll pass'. If he was having a break from work – because in his job, he'd work very long hours, partly away from home, but with some long rests between – he'd see it as a chance to go drinking with the other men, and generally having a good time – even flirting with other women – when he could easily have lent a hand around the house. Like Uncle Ig does for us now."

"That must have been very annoying," I admit. (But it still seems a bit extreme to get someone killed for it.)

"Well, things went from bad to worse," my mother continues. "The more I tried to point out the error of his ways, the more time he spent drinking and flirting."

"I suppose you drove him to it," I can't help saying. Because I can see how my mother might make someone want to do the opposite of what she says, due to her ordering people around. It's the effect she often has on me, after all!

"Really, Rowan" —she sounds irritable now, but in a way that's a relief – it's more like her normal self— "when you have a husband of your own will be the time for you to give advice on how to run a marriage. And it didn't stop at flirting… Just before my brothers arrived, I found out he'd actually been mating with some girl whose mother kept an inn – one near the henge he was working on, where he sometimes stayed overnight."

"How did you find that out? It might have been silly gossip, even. You know what they say – 'rumour flies, rumour lies'."

"Thank you, Rowan. I can do without the old proverbs, too," my mother says tartly. "It was Anya who told me – of course, that made me more angry than ever."

(It's interesting that she seems to have mainly been angry. Some women might have been upset.)

"In any case," she says, "when I accused him, he didn't try to deny it. Made out it was my fault for being a nagging wife."

"Oh. Do you think you were?"

"Rowan, for the Goddess's sake! Everyone has faults. It's no good giving up on a marriage when you realise your husband or wife has one or two. That's why I didn't want you marrying anyone you met in the romantic setting of a festival – even if he wasn't a Hawk."

"I can see that, Mother. But I think some of us can get a pretty good idea of what someone's like – even with their flaws – in just a few meetings."

"Never mind your in-seeing and far-seeing rubbish now, Rowan. Save that for Jelize! Do you want to know what happened or not?"

"Yes. Sorry. Of course I do."

And I settle more comfortably, with my skirt tucked around me, to show this. Even though I can tell it's not going to be a comfortable story.

"It was the evening before Arvan and my brothers were due to set off to put the final touches to their restoration work," my mother explains. "They were planning to be away for three days, but just spending two nights at their lodgings in the village. My brothers were talking to me as I prepared a stew for us all – the younger one even helping me to chop vegetables. Of course, they appreciated how we'd always had servants to do things like that for us at home – Arvan had always taken it for granted that I'd do most of our housework, the same as his mother did. I'd always got on well with both these brothers, and it just made me think how much more pleasant it was to cook for men who were some help around the house."

"So – where was my father?"

"Oh – out drinking with Bram, and some of their friends from the village. Bram normally tried to have a bit of a restraining influence on him. But he was calling this Farewell Drinking – as if he was going on some great journey."

I can't help thinking that was actually how it turned out. But I don't interrupt.

"Of course, my brothers noticed. The elder one said, 'Your husband has rather a liking for the drink, hasn't he? Though of course he's still an excellent craftsman.' Then the younger one added, 'Don't worry, Raven. We'll look after him for you. And make sure he gets safe home.' I think all my rage at his drinking – and going off with other women – and not doing enough in the house – somehow boiled up in me, like a cauldron overheating. Because I said, 'Don't worry on my account. As far as I'm concerned, I'll be delighted if he never returns!'"

"But you didn't mean it!"

"Well, I did at the time. But not in the sense of wanting something terrible to happen to him. More that if he ran off with some other woman – or just ran off – that after a time, the priestfolk and village elders would agree I could be counted as divorced. Or even widowed. And then…then I'd be free to go home. Only I knew that wasn't likely to happen. Because, for one thing, Arvan was devoted to you. For another, he'd didn't seem like someone who wanted to be free to marry again. More like someone who wanted the excuse of 'I've got to go back to my wife and child' to be as irresponsible as he liked elsewhere. So I went on to say, 'Here I am, stuck with a man I can't respect, who goes with other women and is no help around the house. Can't you see why I wouldn't want him back?' And my brothers looked at each other."

"Goodness!" Even though this is an awful tale, I can't help finding it exciting as well. "I suppose it was a very meaningful sort of look?"

My mother sighs. "Well, I realised it was. Later. All that happened at the time was that Arvan rolled in and we ate. I did see my brothers glancing at each other from time to time. But I thought it was just their way of being annoyed with Arvan on my behalf. They'd always taken my part back home."

(This explains more about my parents' marriage. She'd grown up with men supporting her; he'd been fussed over by his mother, my grandmother. Maybe, without realising it, they expected this to carry on.)

"I wasn't expecting them back till late on the third day. But my brothers rode in after breakfast that day with the news that Arvan had been killed at work, falling from a plank at some height… I thought straight away that didn't make much sense in terms of time. Because with them only a few hours' ride away, that must have happened overnight. But my brothers said there must have been something he went back to fix on his own. And slipped. And broke his neck."

Well! I can see why my mother felt she had something to be concerned about. But still not actual proof.

"So did you ask them any more about what happened?"

"It was difficult at first, because we were all tied up with the bother of funeral arrangements. Arvan hadn't discussed it with his family. But they said they all believed in cremation – returning the body to an ash form and setting the spirit free. Of course, it was very upsetting for your grandmother, as well as a shock for Bram, and your grandfather." (At least she appreciates that – though I think 'bother' was an odd choice of word.) "But we decided it was better to hold the ceremony at the henge, not move the body – after all, it was a sacred site, with priests and priestesses swarming around."

"I remember that! Us all travelling to the funeral. Seeing my father's body, and knowing his spirit had gone. And people explaining he wouldn't be coming back. But really I already knew it."

(If I shut my eyes, I can still see my father laid out on a stone slab, as dark and good-looking in death as in life. The temple folk had already embalmed the body, and it was dressed in crimson and gold. And next I see a great billowing red and grey smoke from the funeral pyre.)

"After the funeral, my brothers said they'd go back with us, then hope to pick up a ship sailing north. That's how they'd come – the horses were only hired."

I nod, that bit making sense. People usually travel by water when they can. There's just too much forest in the middle of Britain.

"But as we were travelling back, I happened to say to my brothers, 'Fancy my husband having an accident like that. He was always so sure-footed! I remember him showing me his wooden walkways across the marshes to the south-west, and how easy he found it to run across them.'"

(That sounds quite nice. As if they did get on well to start with.)

My mother's voice and face become grimmer. "I saw my brothers look at each other in a furtive sort of way. And I said – without even thinking about it – 'It was an accident, wasn't it?' I suppose I expected them to say 'Yes, of course'. Which, actually, they did. But in such a way I knew they were lying."

"So, did you tell them so?"

My mother spreads her hands outward. "How could I? If either of them had admitted anything, then how could I have kept a murder a secret? And yet how could I accuse my own brothers – especially of a crime they might have committed to help me? I did wonder how I could go home with them, with such a burden of guilt between us. And they must have felt the same. Because once we got near to Arvan's village, the elder one said, 'We've been talking to your brother-in-law, Bram. He's a good man, isn't he? He says he'll make sure you keep your home – and his uncle on his mother's side, who's a bit wandering in his wits but good around the house, can move in and help you with odd jobs, as well as looking as if you've got a male protector. I expect you'd prefer that to coming north and having our parents push you into another marriage.'"

"Was that bit true?"

"Well, yes. Except I'd've aimed not to let them. Anyway, my younger brother added, 'And maybe you'd like to take up a trade in your own right. Bram says one of his aunts is skilful with herbs, and would be happy to teach you all she knows.'"

(I always knew my mother had become a herbalist for practical reasons, rather than some great calling towards it. This proves it!)

"They did say they'd be back," my mother says – in a final tone, as if she's coming to the end of her tale. "And I thought, in years to come, maybe we could put what had happened behind us, and be on easy terms again. But –

maybe they were afraid I'd accidentally give them away if we saw more of each other – they never did come."

There's a pause while we both look across to the westerly hills. Then I say, "I can see it was difficult – if you thought your brothers had killed your husband – and for me too. I mean – my father and my uncles! Although I still don't think that's any reason for me to stay away from Hawks in general. And certainly no reason for you not to marry Ezra."

"Well, Rowan – if you feel it wouldn't trouble you to marry into a family on friendly terms with relatives who might have murdered your father – you'd best do as you think fit," my mother says, rather surprisingly. Though she has to spoil it by adding, "If Kelvan's serious about his proposal. He strikes me as someone who could play with women's affections as well as on the harp."

"Just because of the way your marriage turned out isn't a reason to be sceptical about everyone else's chances in love!" I say indignantly. "And what about Ezra? Surely you don't believe he'd run after other women if he was married to you?"

"Well, no," my mother admits. "But how can I marry again, with blood-guilt on my hands for the death of my first husband?"

I consider this. From a practical angle it might not make a difference. But I can understand how my mother feels about it.

"Have you explained to Ezra, though? Don't you at least owe him that?"

"No. And I don't intend to. Rowan" —my mother seizes me by the wrist— "swear by the three names of the Goddess that you won't tell him either."

"All right. I swear," I say. Rather crossly. Because I'd no intention of telling him. I can see it's a matter between the two of them. But I do think it's a bit much – someone who's not really keen on religion herself using it to get a promise out of you. Mind, I still think there may be something I can do – for all our sakes. But first, I have to help Anyanda marry Gerwas. Or, actually, that's the second thing. Firstly:

"Mother," I say, rather plaintively. "I do appreciate you telling me all this. But can we please go and get some breakfast? Right now?"

CHAPTER 18

"Thank you for coming to find me, Rowan," Gerwas says gruffly, after I fill him in on the latest events in relation to his love life. "My poor Anyanda! What can we do?"

"Well, my idea," I suggest (admitting to myself that I'm rather flattered to be asked), "is that we ask Crow to withdraw his offer of marriage. And then there may not be a problem. Because my Uncle Bram was happy for you to wed my cousin. And if there's a bit of gossip about it all, so much the better. Because that'll make Aunt Anya keen to get Anyanda married off before it turns into some sort of scandal."

"That's a brilliant thought, Rowan! How soon d'you think you can go and talk to Crow?"

"Me? Aren't you coming too?"

"Well – I'll certainly walk up to the North Camp with you. And if you think it would help, I'm happy to talk to Crow man to man. But I can't help wondering if it would work better if you sounded him out first, then called me in after. More tactful."

I can see what Gerwas means.

"And," he adds, "you are his friend's girl. And I think sometimes these things go better woman to man."

"All right, then."

"And are you ready to go now?" Gerwas asks eagerly.

"Well, my mother knows I'm not working on my stall this morning. I said I needed to take a walk with Kezzie and clear my head. Which – although Kezzie's gone off for a run on the hills now – was true."

Gerwas looks sympathetic. "I suppose you were all feeling upset over what happened."

"Yes," I say, thinking, And you don't know the half of it.

"Do you need anything to eat or drink first?" Gerwas asks. Which I feel is a good sign for Anyanda. He'll make a considerate husband.

"I'm fine," I say. "I had a big late breakfast!"

As we walk towards the North Camp, going uphill at a brisk pace doesn't leave us much breath for talking. But, in any case, we're both lost in our own thoughts. Over mine about Anyanda, and my mother's relationships, I've got a top-layer thought, like a cloak wrapped around the others. And that is: I can't help wondering if Kelvan has said anything to Firethorn yet. It'll be awkward if we arrive just as he's telling her he's got no intention of marrying her…

Asking for Kelvan proves to be the usual magic talisman for getting helpful directions. He may not use the title 'prince', but it's plain everyone in the North Camp knows whose grandson he is! And this time the musicians don't seem so far from the main area of rather grand shelters – just in a kind of glade in a bit of uncleared woodland. As Gerwas and I get nearer, we can hear raised voices. Well, one's more of a yell. Which sounds like Firethorn. And although the difference in accents between ours and theirs is more pronounced with people losing their tempers, I can tell she's saying:

"And you needn't think you can insult me like this,

Kelvan Windhawk! Thinking you can offer me marriage while you pay attentions to other women behind my back." (This is a bit strange. Not what I expected to hear her say.) "At least Mart had the decency to let me know about your little games. So don't think you can come crawling to me for forgiveness!"

"As you say, I'm a Windhawk. We don't crawl," Kelvan snaps. "And you know yourself that our marriage would be more to do with joining our estates than love."

"That sort of thing is for those lower than us in society." (She's not actually shouting now. But she still sounds pretty angry.) "Only, from what Mart tells me, you think you can have both!"

"Well, yes. Of course I do," says Kelvan, in the light tone which sounds typically him. "A man can't be expected to do without warmth – and loving…"

"And I suppose your little Dragon friend sets you on fire?"

"Well, yes. She rather does."

"She looks like the sort who'll shrivel you up if you don't take care. And what sort of powers has the girl got, to be so friendly with a lynx?"

"Rowan's powers have nothing to do with this," Kelvan says determinedly.

"They have! She's bewitched you from the path of duty!"

"What, in not wedding you?" Kelvan asks contemptuously. "She's not the first young woman I've amused myself with. And certainly won't be the last."

"You're impossible!" Firethorn screeches. "Mart – take me back to my shelter. Now."

Gerwas and I are in her path as she storms out of the glade – dragging Mart rather than leaning on him. She glares at us and gestures 'move'. But we don't.

"A 'please' would be nice," Gerwas remarks. "Or don't they teach you any manners up north?"

Firethorn stamps her foot and veers round us. Mart follows – winking, and raising his hand in a half-salute as he goes.

Kelvan, Crow and Sparrow appear at the glade's edge. They stand for a few moments, arms around each other's shoulders, waiting to make sure Firethorn's really on her way. And now they take the few paces needed to join us.

Kelvan takes me by the hands and swings me round. "Well, Rowan," he says cheerfully. "What did you make of that for a performance?"

"Oh," I say cautiously, "that's all it was, then?"

Kelvan laughs. "Of course! You surely didn't think I meant it!"

"Not really," I reply – glad Kelvan's not hurt by my lack of trust, but thinking he needn't find it funny. "It was just that you sounded so convincing."

"That!" Kelvan snaps his fingers. "It was all something Mart and I planned on the way back to camp last night." (So it *was* Mart I saw lurking around behind us.) "And it was all due to what you said, Rowan – about Firethorn and her pride. We hit on a way to make her decide she didn't want to marry me. And in a way that might make her appreciate Mart more. You know – never looked at another girl. And actually, he hasn't."

I think Firethorn's lucky – Mart knows she's not a very nice person, but he still thinks she's the other half of his shell. Some of us might prefer not to join our half at all.

"Well," Gerwas says, with a kind of grudging admiration, "you managed it pretty well between you."

"We are used to an audience," Kelvan says airily. Then, as he seems to take in more fully that Gerwas is with me, "And – Gerwas, isn't it? Are you visiting with Rowan for the pleasure of our company? Or is there something else you want?"

"He does want to ask a favour of you. Well, Crow in particular." I gesture towards the dark glade. "Can we sit down to talk?"

We sit in a semicircle. There's something about it that feels ominous to me. But at least it's out of the wind, which has sprung up and cleared the clouds. After we've explained the situation – well, I have, with a bit of help from Gerwas nodding, mumbling and looking beseechingly at Crow at the right moments – there's a short silence. Then Kelvan says to Crow, "Hard luck."

"Yes, I'm sorry too," Sparrow agrees. "But sometimes loving someone can also mean letting them go."

That sounds almost like a line from a song. But it's still a good point. And it's natural Kelvan and Sparrow's first thoughts are for Crow, their band member and blood brother. But at least they both seem to accept that Crow needs to give up on my cousin.

"Anyanda really is ever so sorry," I tell Crow. "She knows you're an extremely nice person." (Well, I think I can assume she does. And I can hardly say 'she likes you, but not the idea of mating with you'.)

"I'm sorry too, my man," Gerwas tells Crow. "See, it's just that Anyanda and I always knew – from when we met on the road here – that we were, um…"

"…The other half of each other's shells," I suggest.

Gerwas nods eagerly. "Rowan's right. It's just that we let stupid misunderstandings and pride get in our way." (More on her side. But I'm not saying.) "And now," Gerwas says determinedly, "we know where we stand with each other. And what we want to do. Only with her parents guarding her – even if Crow kindly withdraws his offer – are they going to let me anywhere near her? I know Bram, her father, would, left to himself. But her mother might want us kept apart. Sort of – Crow for a husband, or no husband."

"Well, I've got an idea how to get round that," Kelvan says. "Just came to me now while you were talking, Beaver man."

We all look at Kelvan expectantly. His blue eyes are sparkling, as if he's got something adventurous in mind.

"Only, Rowan," he tells me, "I think you'd best leave us. Just while we discuss tactics. I know you can keep your mouth shut." (I suppose that's thanks to the intelligence-gathering discussion.) "And Bram's not the kind to beat information out of his daughter. But I still think it's safer to leave this as men's business."

I'm not pleased. But…

"All right, then. Since it's to help Anyanda."

"It shouldn't take us long," Kelvan explains. "Can you come back and join us for the midday meal?"

"No, I'm meeting Jelize for that. Women's business! And I'd best spend a bit of time on the stall…"

"But afterwards? Because once we've arranged everything for your friend and cousin, you and I can start making our own marriage plans!"

Jelize and I are enjoying our noon meal. We've already established that a little sun-catching hillock is a good spot for it, and Kezzie joins us as we're eating. We haven't talked about anything serious – Jelize is a great believer in not letting outside problems interfere with food, which you should just give thanks for, enjoy, and digest properly. But now, as I'm eating berries – blissful to be doing that in the sun, with Kezzie licking the juice from my chin – she says, "I've seen there was no one on your stall, Rowan. You could have asked me if you wanted some help with it, you know. Even if I needed instructions first."

I look thoughtfully at Jelize. It suddenly strikes me she's maybe feeling at a bit of a loose end – like a spare thread in weaving – when she's not attending extra religious services. Of course, most folk who aren't here on business treat the week as a holiday – with a bit of sacred ritual thrown in. Like the clay-workers do. Or Gerwas, who apparently makes arrows back home. But sports are like a second trade to him anyway, so he's been enjoying all the chances for it here. But without her school, and her plants and chickens to tend (she's asked someone she trusts to look after them), she might like more to occupy her.

"Well, maybe you can do that this afternoon. I've promised to go back to see Kelvan."

Jelize raises her eyebrows. "So you were seeing him earlier? Have you settled your marriage plans?"

"We've cleared the way for them," I say cautiously. "But really I went with Gerwas to see him and the other musicians. To sort things out for Anyanda."

"And how did you get on?"

"Well – Crow's agreed to withdraw his offer. And then Kelvan sent me off because he'd thought of a plan to help further, and with me being part of Anyanda's family it was safer if I didn't know." I bite into an apple. "I'll admit I was cross. But I can see he was right. Because I'd never say anything on purpose. But I might do it accidentally."

"If Kelvan's taken charge, that sounds hopeful for Gerwas and Anyanda. But how's Crow feeling?"

I've not thought a lot about this. "I guess he's just accepted the situation."

"He's taken it very well, then. Some people would say the agreement to wed was binding, and he could hold her to it. Whether he really cares for your cousin, or whether it's more about vanity, it must have been quite a blow to him. But I dare say Kelvan will keep an eye on that."

"Are you saying Kelvan can't trust in Crow's support?" I ask bluntly.

Jelize spreads her hands. "I don't know. But I'm sure Kelvan will… Only, how do you think it will work out for you, being married to such a natural leader? You've got tendencies that way too. Not that that's a bad thing in itself."

"I don't see a problem," I say, surprised. "After all, we'll have separate trades. Him a harper, me a weaver."

"Rowan – I don't want to go casting a stone into a calm pool. But is that going to be Kelvan's long-term aim? Or is the music going to become more of a part-time thing while he goes back to being a warrior prince?"

"Well, that is the difficulty," I admit. "You see, Kelvan wants to carry on being a full-time musician. And he believes Mart would be better suited to the kingship. I can see why, too. Mart's very interested in politics. And he's fallen in love with someone who'll be a hand-in-glove fit for that way of life."

"Well, that's good. I just hope our present king is more easily talked round than folk say is usual with him. Because on the surface your Kelvan does seem suitable. All dash and fire and quick wits. And the ability to manage other people by charm."

Yes, it's that last bit I'm not so keen on. He's so good at putting on an act, I almost believed those things he was saying to Firethorn. But on the other hand…

"Just for those reasons, I think he'll be able to get round his grandfather. Even if no one else can. But, Jelize – there's something else I want your help with. Can you arrange another meeting with the High Priestess for me? By tomorrow morning, if possible?"

Jelize looks at me and nods slowly. "I think I can. But, Rowan – are you sure this is something you want?"

Kezzie nudges up to me in a comforting, encouraging sort of way.

"Yes," I say firmly. "It's about something that might help my mother. And Ezra. And, in a way, me too. So I've got to try."

CHAPTER 19

"Rowan!"

I hear a voice – one with a foreign accent – calling my name as I make my way uphill towards the North Camp. I turn, and see it's that nice black man coming up on my right who works for Ezra. I realise I never found out his name, but we were able to have a good talk that time he was guarding my stall. He now manages to explain to me that he's got some free time, and he's buying small gifts for his family. His country's not far from Egypt, which I know is where Ezra's planning to go after seeing his own folk. And he's gone on to point to the ring which he wears on the third finger of his left hand to show he's married, like the Egyptians do, and says "Ezra" with a sad shake of his head. Then "Raven," with a solemn frown. News about my mother turning down Ezra's proposal has certainly spread. So I feel I have to do something! I manage to explain, mostly by gesture, that I'd like to see Ezra in the West Camp feast hall tonight. I wonder if Ezra understands Egyptian writing – that might make things easier. But then I'd have to put together damp earth, a cloth and a stick – so maybe not. And I don't feel I can go chasing after him during his working hours, even if I had time, as he's probably hoping for some extra good sales towards the end of the festival – I wonder if he's met Firethorn yet. But I do want him to know I've got a plan that may help – even if I can't tell him what it is yet. And I can't help hoping, at the back of my mind, that my mother will melt a bit when she sees him. And then I won't have to do anything. But I know that's a slim chance.

Things don't seem to be getting much cheerier now I've met Kelvan, either. He and Crow are sitting chatting in the Gloomy Glade, Kelvan plucking at his harp strings on and off, and trying to tell Crow he'll write a touching song for him about losing Anyanda. But that doesn't seem to put Crow in much better heart. Anyway, they do tell me their mysterious plans are now sorted out. And that Sparrow has gone off for a stroll with Snapper, but they should be joining us soon.

"What about Mart?" I ask. "Is he still trying to console Firethorn?"

Kelvan laughs – rather scornfully. Crow just looks glum – I suppose at the unfairness of his friends having girls and him not.

"He may well be," Kelvan agrees. "On the other hand, messengers have just come in from the north. And the news isn't too good."

I remember how, when I held Kelvan's brooch, I saw his grandfather looking out of the window impatiently, as if waiting for arrivals. Maybe this is linked in with that. "What sort of 'not too good'?" I ask.

Kelvan shrugs impatiently. "Usual thing. Reports of a fleet approaching. Could be from another country. Or just pirate raiders. I dare say Mart's cross-questioning the men who've arrived for more details."

"Aren't you worried, then?"

"Not really. My grandfather's made sure we've built up a really good fleet of our own in recent years. Plus our temple's got a couple of excellent storm-raisers. The best in Britain. And, judging by what we've seen in competitions, from the near Mainland, as well."

I'm horrified. "You don't mean people have *competitions* in starting storms?"

"Well, only in a very small area. With no one else about. That's a better test, too."

"But what about storm *calming*? Does anyone hold competitions for that?"

Kelvan shrugs again. "I suppose there isn't the call for it. No use as a defence. Although if Mart were here, I expect he'd say: Rowan's right, we could use it to combat a rival storm-raiser, if they had one on deck. But they'd only be putting their own lives at risk if they did so. No, all I'm really concerned about is that my grandfather will use it as an excuse to insist we all go home."

"Well – can't you just refuse?"

Kelvan and Crow both look at me in a kind, rather pitying way.

"With his grandfather's armed guards in the camp? He wouldn't be given a choice," Crow says.

"Crow's right. I'm sorry, Rowan, that it'll mean us going straight north from our wedding. But I've talked to my mother about our getting married, and she's highly delighted. So I'm sure she'd look after you well. And throw a huge feast for us when we get home."

I realise this gives me mixed feelings. Because on the one hand, his having talked to Eleri shows Kelvan's sincere; on the other hand, I get a cold feeling around my heart when I think of going north, which isn't just to do with the weather – although the thought of Eleri, who's a truly kind person, and really seems to like me, does warm it a bit.

"So – would you like to come and talk to my mother now?" Kelvan asks. And I'm just starting to agree when

Sparrow turns up with Snapper. And Snapper leaps on Crow.

It's like all the nine Furies being unleashed – but even at this moment, I can tell Snapper's not so much attacking Crow as trying to tear his clothes. And I can see why, when some small, wizened mushrooms come rolling out from a tear in a pocket. And then Kelvan leaps on Crow, gripping him by the throat.

"Why have you done this?" he yells. "You know it's not safe – you know—"

But at this moment, Sparrow and Mart – who've already exchanged a quick glance and moved to either side of Kelvan – grab a wrist each so tightly that he's forced to let go. He turns on the other two as Crow gasps and I move round towards him. I've taken to carrying a herbal drink in a small flask, which my mother says is a remedy against shocks. Which I think we all need around here.

"What do you think you're doing?" Kelvan asks Mart and Sparrow angrily.

"Stopping you from choking Crow?" Mart suggests. He glares at Kelvan, his dark eyes snapping. But he and Sparrow do let go of Kelvan's wrists.

"When you know what we've agreed? When we've all seen what these did to Eag—people we know?" Kelvan asks – with an odd break in his voice before his last word, as he points to the mushrooms, which Sparrow is now picking up. (Snapper seems quite happy to frolic around without trying to eat them himself, and Sparrow makes a bit of a fuss of him, telling him what a good dog he is.)

"And," Kelvan goes on, his voice sounding a bit more level but still quite angry and upset, "you and Sparrow have probably bruised my wrists pretty badly. When we've got a performance tonight!"

"Well, sorry about that," Sparrow says, "but better your wrists than Crow's neck."

"And I can get you some salve from my mother's stall, if you like – it's not far from here," I offer.

But I can tell it's not really about that, even before Kelvan says, without even looking at me properly, "Thanks, Rowan. But I can get something here. Mart – can we talk?"

Mart looks at Kelvan unsmilingly for a long moment. Then he nods, and they walk out of the Gloomy Glade together. By now Crow's slumped to the ground, burying his face on his knees, his long arms wrapped around himself. Snapper comes up to give him helpful, concerned licks. Sparrow touches his shoulder.

"You all right, man?" he asks Crow anxiously.

Crow raises his head. "I suppose so." He adds bitterly, "You'd think Kelvan would understand I wouldn't have traded for them normally – it was only because of Anyanda…"

"Yes," I say hearteningly, "I think you've been very brave and noble about the whole thing."

"Course you have," Sparrow agrees.

"Well, tell that to Kelvan. Unless he calms down, I doubt he'll even let me play with the rest of you tonight."

"He'll have to," Sparrow says firmly. "After all – we can't do without our drummer!"

"D'you think Kelvan really will try to stop Crow playing?" I ask Sparrow.

It's now mid-afternoon. He and I have gone for a long walk with Snapper and ended up on the far west hill, where we'd gone after the archery contest. Kezzie's arrived, and is playing with her dog friend. Just in a couple of days, it seems to have got a bit colder up here – the ridges of earth, like bones, starting to feel sharper through the grass. But it's still a lot better than in the North Camp. Which I realise isn't only about my getting away from the bad feelings caused by the quarrel – it's about generally feeling free. I wonder if

Sparrow feels the same about being part of the whole Hawk setup, but he doesn't realise, having grown up with it; and maybe that's another reason why he wants to go looking for fire-mountains – I mean, to become a special sort of weather-teller.

"Well, Mart and I won't let him," Sparrow says, quite cheerfully. "Because we'll insist Crow does play. And, as you know, Kelvan's not a prince when he's in the band – we all have the same say in decisions – except when it comes to musical ones, because he usually does know best there."

I'm trying to think how I can ask what I want now. But there's no way except to come straight out with it. "Does Kelvan often lose his temper like that?"

"Well," Sparrow says hesitantly, "there were special reasons. See, there used to be five of us who played together. Me, Kelvan, Mart, Crow – and Eagle. He was a harpist too, for his main instrument. Not as good at making up new tunes as Kelvan. But when the two of them played together..." He shakes his head, as if to say 'it was too wonderful to put into words'.

"So what happened to this Eagle? Did he take some of these magic mushrooms?"

"Well, yes, Rowan. A good handful, we realised too late. And before any of us had the chance to stop him, he jumped off a cliff. At least, one of our steep, rocky hillsides that go straight down into a lake on one side. No one knows how deep they are, and they're supposed to have water-monsters in them. But the main thing is the cold... His body was washed up a couple of days later, in a shallow inlet. So at least his family were able to have a proper funeral. But they were angry with the rest of us, because they thought the rest of us must have encouraged him. Which wasn't true. But if they'd not been wary of Kelvan's position, I think they'd have tried to bring us to some sort of trial over it. And our feelings

– of course, we're used to comrades falling in battle. But this… It happened last spring, but none of us have really got over it. Kelvan was extra angry because he and Eagle played so well together. And as it happened during a festival at our local temple, he was able to have all the ways out guarded, and everyone searched. They were in time to find folk who'd got mushrooms on them. Though of course they swore they weren't the ones who had given them to Eagle."

"So what happened to them?"

"Oh, we burnt their stock, then let them go. So you see, Kelvan was quite merciful really. I mean, High King's grandson – he could have had them all killed."

"I should hope he wouldn't have! I mean, no one forced your friend to trade with the mushroom sellers, did they? And dear little Snapper – did you train him to sniff these mushrooms out?"

"No – more the other way round. He used to go for anything someone was carrying that seemed like food. Of his own accord. It took my sister and I quite a time to train him out of it!"

"And why did Eagle *do* such a thing? Didn't he realise the effect it might have?"

"Well, of course, not to the extent it did. But I can imagine him doing it for interest – to see what would happen. Eagle was always pretty daring." Sparrow ends up on a note of fond admiration, and I press my lips together so hard it hurts. I see Kezzie looking towards me in a slightly anxious way, and I smile to reassure her. But I'm feeling so exasperated! I've often noticed how a lot of the boys and men back home think highly of a lot of behaviour which I, and a lot of females, find simply foolhardy. Although I wouldn't say Uncle Bram's like that. But now I can see that young men from the north – including ones who want another man as a life-companion – can be just the same. Maybe they're like that all over the world, even in Egypt. Not an encouraging thought.

"Are you feeling all right, Rowan?" Sparrow asks rather anxiously. (He's quite good at noticing things about people by ordinary means, the same as Kelvan.) "I know it was an upsetting story."

"Well – it is. But it's not so bad for me. I mean, I never knew your friend. But I guess you were all pretty close."

"I was in love with him," Sparrow says sadly.

"You *what*?" This time I'm simply astonished. "Did he know?"

"Oh yes. We felt the same." (I can't help wondering if they'd mated. And if so, how they went about it.) "But we'd only just admitted it to each other. And got as far as kissing." (Well, that answers my question.)

"You know," I say slowly, "I thought you were interested in Kelvan. Or maybe that was Eleri…"

"I suppose Eagle was a bit the same type to look at. Not quite as tall. But same sort of springy step. Very good-looking… I couldn't believe, even with fewer to choose from, that he'd be attracted to an ordinary person like me."

"Well, it doesn't surprise me," I say, indignant for Sparrow. "You're kind, you're funny, you're a good musician. You have bright ideas, and you're brave." (I pause here – wondering if 'fearless' is a better word – it seems to be part of the Hawk way of life, and I'm not sure it's always a good thing.) "That seems a pretty good package to offer someone."

"My sister said something like that – the eldest, the one who'll keep Snapper, if he likes, when I go overseas. But it somehow seems more believable with a new friend saying it. So thanks, Rowan."

"Oh good. And I hope you didn't mind my getting the wrong impression about you and Kelvan."

"No, of course not! Kelvan is a very important person

to me. Just not someone I'd ever want to be married to."

"But you think he'd be all right for me!" I say indignantly. "That's a funny sort of thing to say."

"I don't mean there's any reason why you two shouldn't be happy together. But I've grown up with Kelvan. He's like a brother to me – not quite like he is to his own elder brother from his side. Or even Mart. But that sort of thing."

"You are blood brothers, of course." (This seems to be very important to Hawks.) "And I hope someday you'll find someone new you can fall in love with. And him with you, of course."

"Well, I hope so too," Sparrow admits. "That's part of the reason I want to go abroad. You see, according to travellers' tales, there are some tribes around the Middle Sea who think it's quite usual for two folk of the same sex to fall in love – and maybe stay together for life, as any married couple might."

I think about this one. I hope it's true, for Sparrow's sake. But I can't help seeing a flaw in the reasoning. "Sometimes men and women must get together, though. Or wouldn't these tribes just die out?"

"Oh, I'm sure they still do that. Just that there's more chance of meeting someone special in a place where it's more an accepted custom."

"And I thought you only wanted to find fire-mountains," I marvel. I can't help adding, "And I hope this time you'll find someone sensible."

"Maybe," Sparrow says doubtfully. "But I rather think I like my men exciting. And you must too, Rowan. Or what are you doing with Kelvan?"

Sparrow's remark about exciting men keeps running through my head as Kezzie and I walk back to the West Camp. I've always thought of myself as someone who'd want a sensible man. And that Kelvan was someone who could be both. Sensible – well, compared with a lot of men – and exciting as well. Now I don't feel so sure.

I find Jelize outside our shelter, watching the sunfall.

"Well, Rowan," she says, "I think I managed all right with your stall."

"Oh, thanks. That's great!"

"And I've spoken to the High Priestess."

"Ah." I go still as I drop to the ground beside her.

"She'll see you after breakfast tomorrow."

I feel a bit as if I've just swallowed a stone. But I don't want to go back on this either. I know I'm lucky that, whether because she was once in the priesthood or for some other reason, Jelize can get access to the High Priestess in a way the rest of us can't.

"Thanks a lot," I say sincerely. And if I can't also sound cheerful about it, at least I try to sound as cheerful as I can.

CHAPTER 20

"Rowan – what's Ezra doing here?" my mother hisses at me.

"He's got a right to come to our feasting hall!" I hiss back. "And I invited him. Because I want to talk to him."

"There's a fine way to repay me! After all my kindness in saying I won't oppose you marrying a Hawk. If you must."

"I didn't realise it was some sort of favour I need to pay you back for," I mutter. "I thought you were just being fair-minded."

(I force myself not to add 'for once'.)

My mother gives a horse-like snort and turns away from me. I wonder if she'll want to change seats. But I guess she'll think, Why should I?

"Your mother doesn't seem too happy to see me, Rowan," Ezra remarks rather drily.

"Oh, you don't want to take too much notice of her moods," I say airily. Which is *true*. Because in case they do get together after all, he may as well start to learn there are times when it's best to ignore her. "But I wanted to see you myself. And I guessed you'd be busy trading in the daytime."

"Well, I have been," Ezra agrees. "There's a new young woman in the North Camp – Firethorn. She's a good one to do business with. Too proud to haggle, but she's got a good idea as to what suits her. So we both feel we get a fair deal." He adds, a bit warily, "She's not one of your new northern friends, is she?"

"Well, more of a friend of Kelvan's friend Mart. And maybe a bit more than that by now."

Ezra's eyes twinkle. "Festivals are certainly a place for lovers' meetings." He adds, a bit more sombrely, "Although we don't all meet with good fortune. And I don't just mean me."

He nods towards the top table, where Anyanda's sitting between her parents, looking miserable and sulky. I've not had a chance to see her on her own all day – her mother stayed close to hand while we were changing for the evening meal. She's not good at picking up thoughts without some outward gesture to match, like a change of expression. And the musicians did tell me it was best if I didn't give her any sort of clue which might cheer her up, because then it would only make her mother suspicious. As it is, Uncle Bram's looking rather downhearted (I wonder if he can't help despising himself for not being firmer with his wife), whereas Aunt Anya's looking pretty triumphant – especially when she flicks a glance towards the end of the table near the entrance, on the left as you come in, and can see Gerwas isn't in his usual place among his fellow Beavers. But there's an edginess about her, as if she doesn't feel sure all will go according to her plans. Well, she is quite shrewd in her own way. And, of course, I know she's got reason not to be.

"Well," I say to Ezra, "I just want you to know I'm going to try something that might help you. But I can't tell you about it in advance."

"Is it something you *should* do, Rowan?"

"Oh, it's nothing *wrong*. I don't think."

"And nothing dangerous? You may be thinking I'm inspecting a gift camel's teeth here, Rowan – but I do feel already that you're like my daughter, and—"

Fortunately – because I'm not sure what the answer is to that one at this stage myself – we're all distracted by the entrance of an elegant woman, accompanied by a few servants, who makes her way to the top table, as if to the manner born. I recognise Eleri and think, Well, of course she is.

Eleri's looking around, and as she sees me she gives me a wave and a smile. She carries on, and everyone makes room for her – I see she ends up sitting next to our highest chief to be present – and finds room for those with her on benches either side near at hand. (We all shuffle along a bit so they can fit in.) Then Eleri beckons to me to come up to her. And, rather touched she's bothered to single me out, whyever she's here (can it be part of her son's plot? But she seemed quite in favour of arranged marriages), I do.

She takes my hands across the table and clasps them warmly. "Rowan – I'm so happy that you and my son Kelvan wish to marry."

"So you do give consent?" I ask, returning the pressure of her hands.

"Naturally. And on behalf of the man of the house – his father – too. And I'm looking forward to hearing the young ones play tonight. Will you join us?"

I'd be delighted to. Not only because I like Eleri – my future mother-by-marriage! – but because I can't help seeing Aunt Anya is turning rather green with envy to see me on hand-holding terms with a princess. Actually, she's really green inside. With flashes of purple. But I don't think Eleri notices. It's struck me she's got quite a gift for cocooning herself from things she doesn't want to see; although I don't know how much that's because she's led a sheltered life, or if it's just her as a person. But I don't want to abandon Ezra, so I say, "Thanks, I'd love to. But I'd best go back to my mother. And my friends."

Eleri nods understandingly. "Of course. And it's hoping to meet Madam Raven later that I am. Another reason to be here tonight. After all, you'll have a lifetime of sitting on high tables once you're wed!"

I walk back to my seat. Slowly. Eleri's suggestions – though plainly well meant – give me a slight feeling of dismay. For one thing, I don't trust my mother to be pleasant. She'll probably make disparaging remarks about Eleri's embroidery – or Hawks in general – or both. For another, it's brought home to me that a prince's wife will be expected to take a certain place in society. Not one I'm sure I want. It's different for Eleri, who's grown up to it. But now the musicians are coming in. So I shake off my concerns and prepare to listen.

"Your Kelvan's certainly in good voice tonight," Ezra comments to me during a short break and, for Sparrow, change of instruments, after the first couple of songs.

"Well, yes," I say cautiously, "and I think they're all playing well."

Which is true. The four of them all seem to be even better than usual. I can feel there's something between them, as if they're all being held together by tight bowstrings. I'm not sure whether that's a good thing in itself or not, and I wonder to what extent they've made up the quarrel. Crow's certainly hitting the drums with a lot of firmness and spirit – and I'm sure Kelvan's looking a bit more at the feasters and less at his friends than he did when playing before. Sparrow's behaving more as usual, but I can tell he's a bit on edge. Mart – well, I never can tell what he's thinking or feeling, either by outward or inward means. But I guess whatever stress is affecting the others will have some impact on him, too.

"Hey, lads – do one of your funny songs," one of the Beaver lads yells when we get to another short pause.

This actually seems to cheer up the musicians themselves.

They grin at each other. Then Sparrow and Kelvan step so they're facing each other, sideways on to the high table. And they start a song where they insult each other in turn.

I know there's a big tradition for this up north. They certainly fall into it naturally; and the other two add the odd drum-roll, or twang of harp string, to chime in with it. Some of what they're singing – well, kind of chanting at each other – is a bit rude. I can see my mother frowning – of course, she's not easily amused by nature. And even in the firelight I can see Aunt Anya's lips pursed together – only she always likes to pretend she's made of finer clay than everyone around her, as if she's an easily shattered beaker. Everyone else is laughing no end – including the man who complained about modern music last time. Jelize is too, which makes me feel it's all right for me to do so. And even Uncle Bram and Anyanda are raising half-hearted smiles.

And now the two musicians are starting to get quite personally insulting to each other. Which I know is part of the tradition, although I don't think it's a good part. Sparrow says something to Kelvan about spoilt rich boys (but aren't all Hawks?). And he caps this by reciting:

"Yes, that's me. Someone who's even more bullied by my grandfather than the rest of his subjects!"

For a moment, there's a shocked silence. You can almost feel it running around the feast hall. And I know I must do something to calm things down. So I start laughing as if it's just a light-hearted remark, not to be taken seriously. And a few other folk, thank the Goddess, are picking up on this and joining in – Jelize near me, Eleri up top, then plenty of others. Especially those where the mead fumes going round in their heads make them a bit unsure what was said in the first place.

Sparrow takes the chance to reply with a remark insulting to Kelvan but not mentioning the king. The other two circle round, and they're now going into a bit of four-sided repartee – clever, that.

"Rowan," Ezra murmurs in my ear, "did Kelvan just say something insulting about his father's father?"

"Well, he did, rather," I admit. "But I hope no one will take it seriously."

"Hmm. It'll be thanks to you if they don't… Although it looks as if we're going to have something new, to take our minds off it…"

Because Kelvan's now walking away from his friends, and near to where I'm sitting. He smiles around charmingly, and says, "And now for a change. I'm going to play for you on my own. And it's going to be a love song!"

The hall falls silent – as much as it ever does. Apart from the man on Ezra's right, who's mumbling complaints into his beard. I'm glad we're not from the same settlement, even if he is a Dragon. But most folk seem just expectant. In an enthusiastic way. And, taking his harp in his hand, Kelvan starts to sing.

> *There's a girl who's stolen my heart*
> *I've looked for it everywhere*
> *How can it be that I'm still walking*
> *With no heart in my body?*

For the first verse, he's turning around to different sides of the hall as he plays and sings. So I'm just taking it as a general love song in the modern, non-rhyming style. And I think how well the words match the plaintive notes Kelvan's strumming on the harp. Plus, because I'm still waiting for him to do something to help my cousin, I'm tending to put anything odd in his behaviour down to some possible plan. But now – to my surprise – he's not only turned to face me, he's coming up just on the other side of me at my table as he sings:

And with that, he puts his harp down. Carefully, on top of some rushes, not just bare earth. But it's still a relief to see he can do that. Sometimes I think the harp's attached to him like a third arm! Now he's sinking to one knee and fishing something out. Maybe he realises bringing his head level with the table looks a bit foolish, because he stands up again. And looks into my eyes. It's one of those moments when there doesn't seem to be anyone but us in the world. Even when I know really that we're in a crowded feast hall. And – oh, Kelvan, what are you doing? – he's holding something out to me. I can see it's a chain with an amber jewel gleaming in the firelight. And it's carved in the shape of a heart.

"For you, Rowan," he says simply. "Will you take it?"

I stand up, and we both lean across the table so he can slip the chain over my head. I don't feel like my ordinary self at all. I feel as if I'm in one of my flying dreams. Only as if this time I've got real, rustling wings.

Then Kelvan turns around again, and the other musicians join him in some kind of chorus to the song.

"I thought you'd like it," Ezra murmurs in my ear as I sit down again. "I let Prince Kelvan have it practically for free."

I finger the amber heart, feeling a bit dazed. Although that could be the effect of firelight, torchlight, and talk in the hall, too. I'm very glad this is a new necklace: because, to judge by my experience with the brooch, Kelvan's family possessions are overcharged with meaning. Kelvan doesn't seem particularly affected by it – he's probably not that sort of person.

Looking sideways, I see Mart and Crow have gone up to the top table – still playing a bit, as if this is part of their performance. Kelvin and Sparrow are still in the middle of the hall, but they've gone into one of their bantering songs again, Sparrow teasing Kelvan about being sick with love. Mart's going behind Anyanda and whispering in her ear. My aunt looks pleased, as if she's getting a new hope up. Of course, she doesn't know anything about Firethorn. Suddenly there's a shout and a thunder of hooves, and Gerwas gallops into the hall – he's riding the trusty pale mare I've already met with the Beavers.

Gerwas races towards the high table, and stops just before it. Mart swings Anyanda over the table to Crow. Crow catches her and passes her to Sparrow, who's waiting to help her up on the horse. Gerwas leans down to offer a hand, and in an instant Anyanda's up in front of Gerwas. They wheel round and head for the door as everyone's staring open-mouthed.

"I'm being abducted," Anyanda shrieks delightedly over her shoulder. "Don't anyone follow us!"

But of course they do.

CHAPTER 21

Gerwas and Anyanda are out of the hall in what seems like a flash of lightning. The first people to head for the doorway are a bunch of young men from the Beaver tribe – I guess, friends of Gerwas, whom he's asked to block anyone who gets in the way. But after that, it's as if most of us in the hall, especially the younger ones, are seized by a kind of tide – like bits of wood in a river surge – and we're all being swept along together. Of course, I want to see what's happening anyway – after all, Anyanda is my cousin. We all shout best wishes from the doorway, waving them on their way as that kind, steady mare canters down a little path and then up towards the western hills. We can even see the flicker of a crimson neck warmer in the dusk which Anyanda's waving to us. (Of course, I wove it, and for a moment I wonder if I could present myself as a good weaver for runaway brides and their men – 'her work is strong yet colourful and attractive-looking, ideal for elopements'.) But then they go round the base of a further hill, and they're lost to our sight.

I realise Uncle Bram is behind me, and he's waving the happy couple off too. "Well, Rowan," he says, tugging at his beard – but in a cheerful way. "I see I've acquired an enterprising son-in-law." He adds, with a twinkle in his eyes, "And, of course, my daughter's been blessed with an enterprising cousin!" Then he turns to head for the hall.

I realise I'm standing near Kelvan and the other musicians, who've come up behind me. They're all hand-slapping and back-thumping each other at the success of their plan. To be fair to Crow, he seems just as lively as the others. I suppose he feels if this had to happen, at least he's played an active part in it.

"Well, Rowan," Kelvan says enthusiastically as he notices me noticing them, "we said we'd help your cousin and your friend to marry. And we've done it!"

"Yes – thanks so much. To all of you."

"Of course, Gerwas's tribal brothers helped too," Kelvan admits. "Still, it's a bit of a triumph!"

"You've all been wonderful," I say warmly. "Only..." I glance a bit nervously back into the hall. "I suppose I'd best go and see how the rest of my family are taking it."

"We're all going in to drink to the happy couple. If your aunt's being difficult, come and join us when you've soothed her down. Only I don't think she'll make too much fuss – not with a princess at her table."

Which shows Kelvan has a fair measure of Aunt Anya. But he doesn't know her like I do. When she's in a bad mood, she's not likely to take any notice of titles – or of a gentle person like Eleri.

So I turn to follow Kelvan and company. But as I do so, I bump into a tall young woman with tears trickling down her cheeks. And I recognise Gerwas's sister.

She recognises me and tries to choke back her feelings.

"Sorry," I say as she looks down on me. "I didn't mean to knock up against you. It's just that everyone's pushing..."

My attempt at light talk, and extending a branch of friendship, seems to cut no ice with her. "I suppose you're pleased about this – maybe helped plan it," she says in a low and furious tone.

"It was my friends who helped. But yes, of course I'm pleased," I say firmly. Adding – because I can't help being curious – "Why, aren't you? Don't you want your brother to marry the woman he loves?"

Brushing her tears aside, she says, "Not if it's to her! I raised Gerwas after our parents died from marsh fever – turning down men who thought I should foster him out. We used to be like this"—she links a finger from each hand—"and now he's gone off with a flighty, self-centred piece who'll completely push me out."

Hmm, there's no denying Anyanda could be a pushing-out sort of person. But as the folk around us straggle back into the hall, I say, "It doesn't have to be like that. My cousin does have a good heart. And she truly loves your brother. Look how she gave up the chance to marry a Hawk! One from a well-off family, at that. And I think she might be lonely for female company at first – she's grown up used to me being always around. If you seize the chance to take her under your wing – get her used to your customs, even if they're not much different from ours – maybe you could become friends. And aren't you planning to get married yourself?"

"Yes – but – he's a good man – but older…"

"I can't help you decide about that. You could live on your own. Or look for someone else. Or both. But if you do like him enough to marry him, I reckon you should throw yourself into it with a whole heart. Then you'll have your own man – and maybe babies – to think about."

"Rowan – the girl due to wed a handsome prince – that's easy for you to say," she jeers. But actually in quite a friendly fashion. And we walk back into the hall together.

It has given me a strange feeling, though, to hear her say that. I've been so used to the people in our village considering us a bit odd. Including Jelize, but it's as if, because she's an ex-priestess, she's allowed to be. Whereas my mother and I being keen on our independence, making our own livings, even having a home a little out of the way – people accept it because we're related to their head man, even if not by blood. But I've always known they gossip about us behind our backs. Now I realise that by marrying Kelvan everyone will start seeing me as an inner-hearth-circle and top-table sort of person. Which is never how I've seen myself.

But I've no time to worry about it now. Because when I get further inside the hall, I can see people clustered around a woman who's sitting down on the middle of the floor. It's Aunt Anya, and she's throwing a huge fit. (Although Uncle Bram's ignoring her and chatting quite cheerfully to other men at the top table – it looks as if they're raising their beakers to the runaways.)

"At least, Madam Anya, let me get you a cushion," Eleri's saying in her soft, pretty voice, as I join them. "It's no good you'll be doing yourself by sitting on the cold earth."

And she gestures to one of her servants to bring round one she must have brought for her own use. Aunt Anya flounces up enough to sit on it. Then starts weeping and wailing again.

"Anya," my mother says firmly, getting out one of her bottles with a herbal remedy, "drink some of this. It'll do you good."

Aunt Anya waves it away (well, I can't blame her for that – some of my mother's potions taste foul – though some folk believe that's to do them more good.) She cries out, "How can your herbs help me at a time like this? My daughter stolen away by a Beaver!"

My mother says coolly to Jelize, "Do you think we should try another remedy? Maybe send for some water to throw over her?"

"That could work," Jelize agrees – gravely, but with a twinkle in her eye. "However, I have heard that some cases of nervous disorder can be helped simply by giving the sufferer a good slap."

"And, Madam Anya, you may not have heard your daughter quite rightly," Eleri says anxiously. "She did mention abduction, but in a cheerful way. And forbade anyone to follow her. So we know she was being carried off willingly. Indeed, my son and his friends would never have helped otherwise."

I can see my mother and Jelize trying not to laugh – dear Eleri's so sincere in thinking Anya genuinely wants reassuring on this point. Before my aunt can say anything even she might regret later, I exclaim, as if struck by a brilliant flash of lightning, "Jelize – would you mind giving me one of your feathers?"

Jelize – who tends to use objects she finds in nature for her adornment – bends her head so I can pull one from her headdress. I stick it into a candle flame, then pull it out quickly, blow the light out and stick the singed, burning feather under Aunt Anya's nose. She splutters crossly, and coughs. But she stops raving.

"Now there's a good idea," Eleri approves. "Rowan's a quick-witted young woman, isn't she?"

Jelize smiles, rather wryly. "Rowan's that, all right," she says.

CHAPTER 22

The sun this morning looks weak and small. Which is how I feel as I make my way towards that small chapel where we had the early-morning service.

As I enter, I see she's waiting for me. Sitting on a plain wooden chair without any of the elaborate carvings I saw in that vision of Kelvan's grandfather's room. But she still looks impressive, with her hooded eyes, and her hands lying still in her lap. As if she's one of those people who don't need fancy clothes or furniture. And her wrinkled face makes her look like some old carving in her own right.

"Greetings, Rowan," she says, in her deep, rather gravelly voice; then, pointing to a stool, "Be seated."

"Thank you," I say, pulling it up so I can sit near her. But not so close I have to look up at her adoringly. I want this to be more a conversation of equals. "I need," I say steadily, "to find out about something that happened a long time ago."

"Rowan – you need to be more exact. Do you mean within recent years? Or many ages ago – say, when Britain was still joined on to the Mainland?"

"Oh, not that far back," I say hurriedly. "Actually, it was something within my lifetime."

She purses her lips. "And what sort of something? It will be hard to tell if I can help you, if you keep that a secret."

I sigh. I realise this may be true.

"Well – I want to know whether a man was killed in an accident. Or on purpose. Do you need to know any more?"

"Not necessarily. But did you think I would be able to give you an answer just because I am your High Priestess?"

"Oh, no," I say, a bit surprised. "It was more something I think I could do. With your help."

There's a glint in the High Priestess's eyes. I can see I've caught her attention, and that from here on our talk's going to be on a new, more serious note. But all she says is, "And why do you think that?"

I draw a long breath. "Well – I know can see something going on at a distance, if it's happening now. And I dare say a lot of people can do that – say, about someone they care for – and animals too, like the way Kezzie and I can send each other pictures—"

"Ah – Kezzie, whom Jelize stole from the temple?"

"She didn't steal her," I say hotly. "She rescued her!"

"You know, Rowan, I deplore the practice of animal sacrifice myself, and have worked to reduce it. Surely it should be obvious that righteous living is what the Goddess requires of us? However, I intended your Kezzie, as you named her, to be a temple attendant. And had an operation performed to save her from having cubs. But she proved too much of a free spirit for our disciplines—"

"Like I'd be!"

The High Priestess smiles faintly.

"Maybe. The point is, it was only some of my fellow devotees who started talking about sacrifice—"

"Just because Kezzie scratched them or something, I suppose. How mean!"

"But I told the others that Kezzie must have managed to

slip her chain. When I knew full well she'd gone with Jelize when she left."

"Ezra says some folk in his home country say the same," I agree. "About good living, not sacrifices. Although they call the Goddess 'Yahweh'. And some of them think of Her as a Him. But in any case, we should be caring more for other creatures than we do. Jelize says we've broken a contract between us, and—"

The High Priestess holds up a hand.

"I know your aunt's views well," she says – but sounding quite affectionate towards Jelize. Whom she's still calling my aunt. "To go back to your point, Rowan – were you trying to tell me you can far-see those in whom you have no special interest?"

"Well, I did recently," I explain. "It was" —I decide there's no harm in telling her— "someone I didn't know or care about. Except for him being Kelvan's grandfather."

"You mean, his father's father? The king?"

(She sounds quite alert now.)

"Yes, that one. But he realised I was looking in on him – not that he knew who I was, of course. And he got angry. So I stopped."

"And how did you do that?"

"Oh – I just drew a sort of mist down between us. Why? Was there a way I could have done it better?"

I'm asking because the High Priestess looks a bit perturbed. But she actually gives a faint, rather rusty-sounding laugh. "No, Rowan. I'm just intrigued you could do it untaught. I know it was never one of Jelize's gifts. So, I take it you want me to help you see a past event. Is that it?"

"Just it," I nod, pleased she's understood.

"In this instance with – shall we say, a friend's grandfather – can you pinpoint anything which led to your having that vision?"

"Oh, I'm sorry. I didn't explain. It was Kelvan's grandfather's cloak-brooch. When Kelvan gave it to me to hold. I think, because his grandfather's a powerful man – in himself, not only because of his position – that somehow got into the brooch. Only Kelvan doesn't feel it particularly, except to annoy him a bit. And that might be because the brooch is old-fashioned, and he likes modern things."

"Yes," the High Priestess agrees rather drily, "from what I've seen of young Prince Kelvan, that sounds very likely. So, with your quest – do you have any possession of this man who's gone to Spirit?"

"No, I don't," I say. Rather bitterly. I feel this is a score against my mother. My father had a gold armband with fancy designs. He used to let me run my fingers over it. But I'm sure it wasn't on his body at the funeral. Did she take it to trade with? Or, to be fair, did she give it to his family? But I can't ask her. And if it's back in the village, Bram might say. But that's no good, because I need to do this now.

The High Priestess looks deep in thought. Then she turns her hooded eyes back on me. "It is possible to find a new object you can use. But you'll have to put the power into it yourself."

"How do I do that?"

"You'll need to go on a journey."

"But I need to find out what I can before the end of this festival! It matters for what my mother – and I – and other people decide to do. With our whole lives."

She holds her hand up again. "Not a bodily journey, Rowan. One in spirit. And that's where I and a few sisters I trust" —I suppose she means priestesses— "can help. If you return tonight, we can provide a herbal drink that will put you into a state of trance. And use incantations to help you return to your body when the time is right."

"That sounds good. I mean, some folk say we can leave

our bodies when we're asleep anyway. I've felt that a bit. Like with my dreams about Egypt."

"That's true. But this will be a longer parting. And you have to know – there is a slight chance the person who undergoes this ritual may not return! However," she adds reassuringly, "that's why we'll be there. To make sure that doesn't happen."

That sounds all right, then. Because I wouldn't try this if there was a stupid risk. But after the High Priestess has given me her blessing and I've stepped out into the now-bright sunlight, I find Kezzie and Jelize waiting for me a little anxiously. So we sit down nearby, Jelize and I on our cloaks as it is quite chilly, and I tell them about the meeting.

"Rowan – I'll be there tonight," Jelize says, in a determined sort of way.

Kezzie rubs up against me, and looks at me anxiously.

"I wouldn't expect you to come," I tell her, ruffling the fur on her neck. "I know it'll be fine if Jelize is there. Only – Jelize – will the High Priestess let you come? After all, you gave up being a priestess years ago."

"Oh, that shouldn't be a problem," Jelize says confidently. (I've noticed before how little in awe she seems of the High Priestess, compared with most folk, but this is more – almost as if she can make a demand of her.) "I'll go and see her about it now."

It's a pretty boring afternoon on my stall. Some festivalgoers have given up shopping and have gone to watch 'friendly' feetball matches between the tribes. Which I understand can be quite exciting, but I don't feel that strongly about cheering on the Dragons. Maybe I just want the best players to win – a bit like Gerwas, really. Or it may be because my mother and I have never totally fitted in with the rest of our village, so I don't completely see myself as a Dragon. There again, I'm sure I don't see myself as a Hawk!

Those people who are still going round the stalls are looking for bargains – chances to barter down the traders. But I'm not happy to do this, because I feel it's unfair on all my earlier customers. Plus Ezra advised me against it when we were chatting about some more ordinary things last night. "If you get a name for selling cheaply at the end of a festival, no one will be likely to trade fairly with you at the start." And while I can't help thinking it may be different at his high-quality end of the market, trading mainly with rich people, it's nice he sees a future for me where I'm going round lots of festivals like he does. So even if I have to go to Kelvan's home when we're first married, maybe afterwards...

"Good afternoon, Rowan."

"Anyanda!"

She must have come up behind me while I was lost in these thoughts. She's looking very well. Smug and smiley on the outside, but with an inner- happiness glow too.

"Well," I say, a bit at a loss how to start, "so you're a proper married woman now."

Anyanda laughs. "I certainly am!"

"Mated and all."

"Of course! The first time," she wrinkles her nose, "was a bit fast. But the second time was better. Then this morning – before we rode back to the Beaver camp for breakfast – that was divine!"

(Oh. Right. I hadn't realised folk could mate more than once in a night. Another useful thing my mother, and even Jelize, have *never explained*. Then again, Anyanda's always been a show-off. It's just a good thing she and Gerwas are happy to have babies soon, if they're pushing up the odds for it.)

"Sounds as if you're getting on all right with the rest of Gerwas's tribe, then," I say, to change the subject.

"Oh yes," Anyanda says confidently. "Everyone seems to admire the way we ran off together. And his friends" — she attempts a modest cough— "say he's done well – to catch such a pretty girl."

"And what d'you think your parents have been saying?" I can't help asking.

To do her justice, Anyanda looks a bit anxious at this. "How are they taking it?"

"Well – all right, really," I admit. "Your mother started to throw fits – but when my mother threatened to throw cold water over her, and I stuck a burnt feather under her nose, she stopped."

Anyanda gurgles with laughter. I can't blame her. "What about my father, though?" Anyanda's always been fonder of Bram – which is understandable.

"Pretty pleased. And firm with your mother about it. It sounded as if he'd always favoured the match, so he was glad you'd taken matters into your own hands."

Anyanda's face clears. "Oh, that's good. I'll go and look for him in Beaker Alley now. Well – them, I suppose. If my mother starts being difficult, I'll remind her I'm a married woman!"

"Good luck with that one!"

"Oh – another thing, Rowan. I thought Gerwas's sister might be a bit difficult. Well, you know how she was before. But she had a really nice chat to me at breakfast. Said she hoped she could be an elder sister to me too. And if there was any way she could lend a hand while we were settling into my new home, she'd be happy to help..." Anyanda pauses thoughtfully. "It sounds like she's pretty good at sewing." Which Anyanda dislikes. But if it keeps them friendly, so much the better. I'm glad the sister listened to me.

"I'll miss you, though," I say suddenly. Because thinking about Anyanda setting off for her new life makes me realise this.

"Well, I'll miss you too," Anyanda says – but in an airy manner, as if she's not really too bothered. "But you'll be off – marrying your handsome prince."

"Only don't call him that," I say. But doubtfully, because I don't know if he'll let folk use the title when he's home.

Anyanda shrugs. "Whatever he wants to be called – he and the other musicians were a brilliant help last night. Gerwas has said he'll look out for them at the feetball, to thank them."

"Yes – I think they were going to look on. And play a bit between matches."

"Well, I can't take too long with my parents – got to cheer on my husband's team! But if they are nice, I guess we'll join you for tonight's feast." She pauses and shades her eyes. "Oh, Rowan – isn't that Kelvan coming this way?"

"It is," I agree, surprised. "I wonder what he wants."

Anyanda throws me a saucy glance. "Can't keep away from you, I suppose. Well, I'll be off!"

And with a wave of her hand, she disappears around the back of my stall.

CHAPTER 23

"Rowan – I need to talk to you. Can you leave your stall?" Kelvan asks (although sounding as if he takes it for granted I can).

"Well, Ezra's servant comes from the near Mainland," I say, glancing at the man, "and he speaks British. So I can ask him to tell someone who wants something from the stall to come back soon."

"Yes, you do that," Kelvan says, sounding rather impatient. "Because, Rowan – this is important!"

However, now we've got to a clear space where we can sit down, he doesn't seem in a hurry to start. He's staring across at the horizon of high trees beyond the Big River. The wind's ruffling his dark hair, and I feel like running my hands through it. But that might lead to us kissing. And I want to hear what he's got to tell me.

He says abruptly: "Rowan – we'll need to get married tonight."

"We'll *what*?"

"Yes – my grandfather wants the Hawk camp to set off home tomorrow, not wait for the final feast."

"But you and the other musicians had such great plans

for that! People will be leaving their own feast halls and coming to yours specially to hear you!"

"Yes, well," Kelvan says wryly, "you know my grandfather's views. Music's something we play at. Being warriors and rulers – now, that's our real work."

"But you don't *agree* with him!"

"No, but Mart does," Kelvan explains ruefully. "Sparrow wants to go off on his weather-observing travels. Crow – well, Crow's a bit of a broken arrow at the best of times…"

"But you don't need them! You could make up songs – and sing, and play the harp – on your own. Like I do with my weaving."

Kelvan looks thoughtful. "Of course, some men do," he admits. "And, you said, some women in Egypt…"

"Although I think they play together too. For parties or religious ceremonies. But you could just go off to play on your own. Can't you send a message with the others and say that's what you've decided to do?"

"And have my grandfather getting intelligence seekers to find me and drag me back? It's not as if music's something you can do quietly – not to make a living out of it."

"All right, then," I say gloomily. "But I'm not leaving until midday. Remember, it's the big weaving competition. In the temple."

"Oh, that," Kelvan says vaguely. "I guess it has to be then from the religious angle – winding up the threads of the festival and all that. And since you're keen, I'll try to work around it. But it's not important for your future, is it? When we're married, we can set up our own household, and you can run that. With weaving for a pastime, if you like."

"Like Eleri and her cushions? But Kelvan – I *want* work of my own. Like I thought you did with your music."

"Well, we can work something out," Kelvan says easily.

"But for now – even if it's going to be a brief ceremony – I think we'd best tell your family."

"Yes, they can do without any more surprise weddings. And I'll need to talk to Kezzie about being ready to leave by noon tomorrow."

Kelvan looks surprised. "Are you expecting Kezzie to come with us?"

"Of course! What did you think she'd do?"

"She and Jelize seem to get on pretty well. And Jelize fetched her from this temple, didn't she? I thought they could be company for each other."

"You don't understand! It's not a bad plan. But Kezzie and I are in each other's hearts. Like you and me, but in a different way. And besides – what about company for me in the north?"

"You'll have me, won't you? And all my family and friends."

"Yes – yours. And I bet they've all expected you to marry a woman from your tribe. Like Firethorn. And the way you're all each other's cousins! Even if you'd married another Green Isle princess, or a chief's daughter from the near Mainland, I reckon you'd be related somehow. The way top table people are."

"Rowan, I think you're worrying too much. Fine about Kezzie, though. I mean, I like her, too."

"And she likes you," I admit. "But another thing – I won't be able to spend our wedding night with you. I've got to take part in this vigil. With some priestesses. Because—"

"You what?" Kelvan leaps up – whole body, not just eyes, ablaze. "This is starting to sound like one excuse after another—"

"But there's a really important reason for this vigil. Just let me explain—"

"I don't want to hear this! Rowan – I don't think we have the same ideas at all about what marriage means."

I'm starting to get cross now myself. "Well, maybe we don't! Because I think if someone's got a special gift, they should use it, not bury it in the ground! I can see it would be difficult for you to become a travelling musician for life. But I can't help wondering – even though your grandfather's a hard man, and the training's tough – you like sticking with what you know. And the comfort – never having to worry where your next meal's coming from."

Kelvan's lips get thin. I can't help noticing that when he's angry, he looks even more handsome than ever.

"If that's how you feel, then it's goodbye," he says curtly. "Because you're right – people did expect me to make a different sort of marriage. But I thought you were worth the sacrifice."

I spring up too. "Maybe it is no good us going on," I say, glaring at him. "Because I don't want a lifetime with a man who thinks he's done me a big favour by wedding me!"

Kelvan raises a hand, as if in farewell. "Well – the Goddess go with you, Rowan."

And he whirls off down the hill, his cloak billowing behind him.

I sit for some little time, thinking about what's just happened, and how it seems as if my and Kelvan's marriage plans have suddenly come unravelled. Part of me's thinking, Surely it can't end like this, while another part's thinking, My parents met at a festival, and found they didn't have much in common – maybe we'd be the same. And at that, Kezzie bounds up and starts licking me with lots of enthusiasm. "Cheer up, cheer up," I hear her telling me. Just as I'm taking time to hug her and lean my head against hers, taking in the comforting scent of her fur, she becomes alert – although not in a danger-noticing way. I look up and see Sparrow making his way up the hill, Snapper frisking around him. And now they've reached us, Snapper and Kezzie run together, and sniff at each other in a friendly way.

"I've just seen Kelvan," Sparrow says, dropping to the ground beside me. He's plainly come prepared not to beat about the bush. "He told me you two had fallen out."

"Was that *all* he said?" I ask cautiously.

"Well, what he actually said," Sparrow admits, "was 'Rowan's being totally unreasonable, I don't think she wants to marry me at all.'"

"Yes, I suppose he thinks not wanting to wed him proves you're hardly in your right senses," I say. Crossly.

"He did say you were refusing to spend your wedding night with him due to some religious vigil. You have to admit, that sounds a bit odd."

"There's a special reason for it! And why I have to do it now!"

So I explain – once I've sworn Sparrow to secrecy – and he listens carefully. Then he says, "Well, I can see why you want to find out the truth behind your father's death. Whatever you do with the information. Especially when it might make a difference to Ezra and Madam Raven – and you, with your uncles in the north."

"Yes – it would make so much difference to what I did if we met. Although I suppose that's not so likely now. I would have told Kelvan all this, but he didn't give me a chance."

"He is pretty quick-tempered. But I think this time he was upset. Underneath. Only I don't know what he'd have made of all this – he's not someone with much of a feel for anything outside our ordinary senses – or maybe it all goes into his music."

"You're not like that, though."

"No." Sparrow puts an arm round me, and I lean back against him as our animal friends play around us. "I can talk to different creatures, and listen to the stirrings of Mother

Earth – but then, I'm not such a good musician."

I sigh. It would have been easier if I could have fallen in love with Sparrow – we've got so much more in common. But apart from him wanting to marry another man, maybe nothing will stop Kelvan being the other half of my shell.

"So," Sparrow says, "do you want me to try explaining to Kelvan for you?"

I think about this one. "Kelvan's very loyal to his friends, isn't he? Even when they don't want him to be – like with you and the archery contest. If he knew there was even a bit of risk to what I'm planning, would he try to stop me?"

"Yes, he might see it as taking a risk when he was doubtful if it would yield a useful result anyway. And I can imagine him committing sacrilege by bursting in on the High Priestess and trying to forbid you from going ahead."

I nod. "Yes. That's just what I mean. And Jelize is supporting me – I reckon she knows a lot more about these things than Kelvan does. I'll tell him when it's all over."

Sparrow looks relieved. "I'm glad you said that, Rowan. Because I've got some news of my own to tell Kelvan. And I'm not sure he'll be too pleased about it."

"What news?" I can't help asking.

"I'm not going back north," Sparrow says abruptly, his arm loosening.

"You *aren't*? But where are you going?"

"Setting off on my travels to the Mainland. I don't think there's any particular season for when these fire-mountains erupt. So I may as well start now."

"Only it sounds like you've just decided—"

"I sort of have. It's seeing the way Kelvan and Mart are just prepared to accept the king's summons. Even if Kelvan doesn't want to. I know I'm not important to the government of Britain. And my parents don't even own a lot of land, like Crow's do. But if I don't make the effort to break away now

– when I'm not too far from the south coast – who knows when I will?"

"I can see that. But it's brave of you – being prepared to go off on your own."

"Well, I won't be that, exactly. To start with, there'll be the two family servants who've been with me at camp. They're a bit old – over thirty – but still pretty fit. Quite fancy the idea. And I'm going to ask your friend Ezra if we can go with his party across the Shallow Sea, at least. After all, they're used to travel."

"And what about Snapper?"

Sparrow glances over to Snapper, now curled up with Kezzie. "I've given him the choice of staying with my eldest sister or coming with me. After I sent him mind pictures of a big boat, he's thinking he'll stay. She's always been as much his person as me. And maybe he's safer this way."

I can't help feeling a bit envious of the way everything's falling into place for Sparrow. Although he deserves it, for his determination.

"Sparrow – do your parents know you want to find a man as a life-companion?" I ask impulsively.

Sparrow smiles. "Well, I've not talked to them about Eagle the way I did to my sister. But in a general way, they know."

"And they're happy with that?"

"Well, they want me to do what's right for me. They've already said they'll pray for me to find fire-mountains, and a nice husband. And come back safely, of course."

"Of course… I'll miss you, though. And if I do end up with Kelvan, I won't have such a good friend in the north."

Sparrow gently squeezes one of my hands. "We can try scrying each other, when we get the chance. But in any case, Rowan – wherever you are, I'll always be your friend."

"Thanks. Well, I'd better be getting back to the stall."

"And I'd best try catching Ezra. But I hope all goes well tonight. And that I'll see you before we strike camp tomorrow."

We both stand, Kezzie and Snapper coming to stand beside us as we give each other a quick hug.

"The Goddess be with you on your journeys, Sparrow!"

"And you on yours!"

"D'you think I'll have some?"

Sparrow looks surprised himself.

"It just came out that way… But, yes, Rowan – somehow I reckon you will!"

CHAPTER 24

I'm walking along a narrow road with steep cliffs on either side and noisy turbulent water in a ravine between them. It's dark overhead, maybe due to clouds as well as the overhang of the cliffs. But whatever gives it this ominous purple-black colour, it's not like anything I've ever seen on Earth. Sometimes there are flashes of jagged lightning, but they only show how slippery and unclimbable the cliffs are. Also, I feel it's all right to look round. But when I do so, I can see the cliffs have somehow shifted so there's always one blocking the path at some distance behind. Which means I have to go on. Also, my left hand is holding a thin scarlet thread, and I seem to know I must follow wherever it takes me.

I'm starting to realise this is the journey I chose to undertake in Spirit. I know it was my decision, but I wonder if putting up a prayer to the Goddess might help. So I do that, and it does, in the sense that an upward path appears in the cliff face on my left a little way ahead. So I reach it and start climbing.

At first the footholds and handholds are quite easy, and the thread is still there to guide my direction. I don't seem to be any better at climbing in Spirit than I was in body. It's not as if I've lived somewhere I'd get a lot of practice, unlike Kelvan and company. But I'm still making progress. To where, I don't know, because the path is diagonal, and the cliffs slant outwards. Then, quite suddenly, it becomes hard. The rocks are sharp – it's like grabbing, and treading on, knives. Instinctively I drop the thread – and almost let go altogether. But at this moment, I hear a voice behind me.

"Come on, Rowan – you can do it! There's a shelf where you can stand round the next bend."

"Jelize!" I cry. "How've you got here?"

"I said I had to come with you. But don't talk – or look round," she says. "Just move!"

I even feel one of her hands pushing my right foot upwards. So I do move. And she's right. I have to press myself against the cliff face, but I can stand flat and upright. As my hands feel for crevices to steady myself, my left one touches a small, rough-feeling chain.

"Jelize," I call, "I've found something!" I turn my head to say this, as I'm also trying to make room for her on the ledge. And so I see her fall.

As this happens, some kind of soft, dark cloud surrounds me, and I can't help sinking into its cocoon-like warmth…

And now I feel rough fur on my hands, and a rough tongue licking my face, a heavy body pressing against me. At least, that's what it all feels like! It's an effort, but I open my eyes. Bright sunlight sifts into the chapel, and the High Priestess is watching me from a chair.

"Kezzie," I say, bewildered, as she purrs joyfully and rubs herself against me. "What are you doing in a chapel?" I look at the High Priestess. "So – I did come back!"

"My child," she replies in her gravelly voice, "it was Kezzie who brought you!"

The High Priestess moves towards me, a small flask in her hand.

"Drink this!"

I do. Although the dark, mysterious liquid makes me cough. There are certainly some strange essences in this that you wouldn't find in any of my mother's straightforward remedies! But it does help me to sit up straight and feel more alert. That's when I realise I'm clutching something small and hard in my left hand. As I uncurl my fingers, I see the small red stone on the chain that I'd pulled from the crevice.

"Did I bring this back with me?"

"Yes. Your finding it by ordeal in spirit made it possible."

I suddenly remember everything. Including Jelize falling. "Jelize! Where is she?"

A wave of grief sweeps across the High Priestess's face. She says simply, "Jelize didn't come back."

"Then – what's happened to her?"

"If you mean to her mortal body – it's being prepared by some of the sisterhood. The cremation will be at sunrise tomorrow."

"But I'd never have done this if I'd known there was a risk to Jelize!"

"You didn't ask her to join you on your quest, Rowan."

"No," I admit. "I think it was because I followed her when she went to talk to this wolf-man – an outlaw chief. But Jelize was always wonderful to me… I can't help feeling as if I've really lost an aunt."

"And I a daughter."

"Oh, of course," I say, trying to be polite, "that's what you called her when she was a priestess, I suppose."

"No, Rowan. That's not what I mean."

She looks at me closely, with those hazy grey-green eyes so like Jelize's, and continues: "Rowan – I'm going to tell you a secret I want just one other person in the world to know."

"If you tell me, Kezzie will know too," I point out.

The High Priestess smiles faintly. "Yes – but she can't repeat it. I'm not going to ask you to swear by the three faces of the Goddess – or that stone you're now wearing – or anything else you might hold sacred. There are some secrets you can only tell someone if you can trust them without binding oaths. But I want you to know that Jelize really was my daughter."

I can only stare. A jumble of thoughts, like tangled wools, are filling up my mind. Like: Does she really mean she was Jelize's blood mother? I thought you weren't supposed to mate if you were any kind of priestess. But Jelize always did seem more at ease with her than the rest of us. And they did have the same colour eyes...

"Can a priestess have a child, then?" I ask. Because this is the point my thoughts have wound up to.

"Well, of course we're not meant to. Apart from those who have children when married, and joined our order in widowhood, when their families are adult. If we did, and it were known, the punishment would be death. Although in practice it's more likely someone would be sent away quietly."

"So – am I allowed to ask who the father was? One of the priests?"

"No, Rowan. It was your grandfather."

I put my head in my hands. Then I look up.

"You mean – my father's father?"

(My mother did tell me once that her parents had both gone to Spirit before I was born. And in terms of where tribes live and everything, it just seems more likely.)

She bows her head. "The same. We met through a summer festival. And we fell in love. It was like a fire running through dry grass. Unstoppable."

She pauses. I can't help thinking, You can damp down a fire if you get enough buckets of water. But she goes on.

"I thought I was past childbearing age. But of course it proved otherwise. I got word to your grandfather that I needed to see him. He managed to visit in the autumn. That's when we agreed – if I could give birth in secret, and pass the baby off as one of the foundlings left to our care, he'd persuade his wife to adopt it."

"Goodness! She didn't know, though?"

"No, we kept that from her. And rightly. When we met again, the flames had died down. I still felt it was my calling to be a priestess. And he was really happier with a quiet, dull woman—"

"If you mean my grandmother," I say indignantly, "she was a lovely, kind person, actually."

The High Priestess smiles in quite a kindly way. "Well – I dare say she was."

"And," the thought strikes me, "Jelize really was my blood aunt!"

Oddly, this thought does give me a bit of comfort. Also, I think of how difficult it must have been if Jelize and Bram were in love. Because there may be countries where men are allowed to marry their half-sister, or have two wives, but there would have been no chance of Aunt Anya agreeing to anything like that – plus Uncle Bram and Jelize might not have agreed with it themselves.

"Did Jelize know? About your being her mother?"

"Later on, yes. And – despite some differences of opinion – we took much delight in each other's company."

That's one nice thing to think about.

"Of course," the High Priestess goes on more briskly, "I'll make sure your Uncle Bram's family are informed. No doubt you'll all wish to attend the funeral."

"Oh – yes. I expect so. And" —I look at the red stone distrustfully— "what am I supposed to do with this?"

"Ah – that's something you'll find out for yourself.

Best hide it under your tunic. And don't you have a weaving competition to go to?"

"Yes – I suppose I'd better," I agree, slipping the chain over my head. It looks very insignificant next to Kelvan's gift, and I do tuck the stone away. What with that, and my shell – admittedly on a short thong – my neck's starting to feel overcrowded.

"Now, Rowan. Do your best. You know Jelize won't want you to give up!"

"No," I admit, "I suppose she won't!"

"I'm sorry, Rowan." The priestess presiding over the weaving places a hand on my shoulder, "We can see your work's very good. But we can't rank you in the competition, because you're the only one who hasn't finished."

"No, of course you can't. I'm usually quicker. I just had some other things to think of…"

"Ah, one of your aunts going to Spirit. We understand. And of course you're younger than some of your rivals." She sweeps a hand around the room (if you can call it that; it's an area of the temple that's open to the sky). "We hold this event each autumn. Maybe another year?"

"Maybe," I agree, feeling unable to think beyond today. "Could I stay to finish, though? Just for its own sake?"

"A gift for the Goddess?" the priestess suggests approvingly.

"Well – I just like the design you gave us. But I'm sure it can be that too."

When everyone else has gone, I lean towards my loom, and the chain slips out, so that the red stone touches my work. I push it back. Then as I look towards my loom again, I see a picture's appeared on the wool. On top of what I've woven. And it's a moving picture! It's like seeing something happening in real life, except with no sound, or anything for the other senses. Of course, in a temple like this you might expect strange sights. But I know this is something to do with me. Because the scene is one of three men laughing and talking at a table. And I recognise one of them as my father.

The three men seem to be getting on well. They're laughing, and playing some dice game in an idle way. Smoke from the fire in this low, dim room keeps blowing back across them. But they just cough a bit and carry on playing. I can see the other two look like each other – and my mother. So I guess they're my uncles.

The place seems to be somewhere you'd go to eat and drink, and maybe spend a night. I can see hangings dividing off other rooms, and groups of different people at other tables. I see a young woman coming up to my father and friends, a jug in her hand. After she's refilled their beakers with what looks like mead, she puts her jug down and ruffles my father's hair. He takes her other hand and whispers something in her ear. His companions are now frowning. And an older woman, who looks as if she's in charge, and might be the young one's mother, orders her away.

The picture disappears, and for a moment I'm just back with my ordinary wool. But now it starts up again…

It's night, with a crescent moon. I can see my father and this young woman standing together on some sort of scaffolding. It's clear they're arguing. She opens her mouth as if she's starting to shout. He's pointing to what I guess is the west, and gesturing as if he's got a child in his arms. She protests again, he shrugs it off. He turns on his heel as if he's about to start climbing down, just as she comes at him, arms flailing. His expression is more one of surprise than alarm as he falls.

Then, with hardly a pause, the scene changes to one where the woman and the two brothers are kneeling beside a figure sprawled across the grass. One of the men looks up from examining the body, and shakes his head. The woman throws herself about hysterically, then grabs the men by a wrist each, as if pleading with them. They look at each other and join hands with her. I can tell as clearly as if it were in Egyptian writing that they're swearing some solemn oath never to tell anyone she was responsible for the death of my father.

Then the picture turns to black, and I know it's the end of the dream-pictures. I look at my loom a bit longer, then finish my task. Which doesn't take long – and I have promised it as a temple gift. I go out, looking for a priestess to present it to. I can tell, looking at the light grey sky, that it's not yet noon. And as Kezzie bounds up to join me, I realise I can go and find Kelvan. Because, now I know my uncles didn't kill my father – and can tell Kelvan how I needed to find out – maybe we can work out our general differences.

So I make for the North Camp, Kezzie close beside me. She seems at ease, but gives me slightly anxious glances every now and then. Which may be because now we've got here, it looks as if most folk have already struck camp. And the remainder are bustling about getting ready to do so. But because of that, the guards aren't too strict: they just nod me and Kezzie past.

As I'm staring about, wondering which person to ask about Kelvan, the man who wanted me to be an intelligence gatherer recognises me. As I do him – I suppose there's not so much of a crowd for him to blend into. He nods in a friendly way, and comes up to us – I think Kezzie recalls his smell.

"Good morning, Rowan Weaver. And lynx."

"And you...she's called Kezzie." I try to stay calm, but can't help adding, "Do you know if Kelvan's gone?"

The man looks at me as if he feels a bit sorry for me. "Prince Kelvan pulled out after breakfast, with most of the others. He did leave a message with me in case I saw you – he knew I'd be one of the last to leave."

"Oh – what?" I ask warily.

"That he's sorry things didn't work out between you. And about one of your aunts – I gather she went to Spirit quite suddenly?"

I nod.

"That's hard. Maybe the heart stopped suddenly? That can happen even to someone quite young who seems well. Did to one of my brothers."

I nod again. Because maybe that is the reason, if not the real one – not what caused it.

"Well," he says, sounding more practical, "if you're no longer planning to marry Prince Kelvan, what about my offer of work?"

"Oh – no thanks." I rub my hand across my forehead. "That was never the reason I refused in the first place."

"Fair enough. I dare say we both want what's best for Britain. In our own ways."

"Well, I sort of do," I say doubtfully. "But I think I'm more bothered about what's best for people in general. Although I do appreciate it was an honour to be asked."

"Ah, well." He raises one hand. "May the Goddess light your path, wherever it may lead."

"Yours too."

I return the salute. Then Kezzie tugs at my skirt, as if to say 'come on, we're done here'. And I know she's right.

CHAPTER 25

"Rowan!" I hear my mother calling as Kezzie and I get down to the woody area below the temple and between the camps. She comes up, looking quite concerned, and thrusts a small bag at me. The knobbly objects inside feel like bread and apples. "You've got to *eat*, you know. However upset you are about Jelize!"

"Oh – yes – that."

I realise by the sky that it's now noon. It's one of those blank days – no sun or rain, just a white sky that looks as if it you could paint on it, as folk do on cave walls. My mother's looking at me as if I've said something odd. Which, to be fair, isn't surprising. Before she can shove some remedy for shock at me, I say, "Mother – I need to explain something to you. Can we sit down somewhere quiet?"

It's quite easy to find a grassy patch where we can spread our cloaks; so many stalls have packed up – even though a lot of folk will stay for the final feast night, and the religious processions that go with it, before departing on the Sun's Day. I'm glad we're some way to the south-west of that place where Jelize and I had a midday meal.

So I tell my mother the whole story. About me and Jelize and the High Priestess, and the weaving vision. All but the bit about the High Priestess being Jelize's blood mother. And I realise I'm quite glad not to tell her that bit. Because I can imagine my mother taking it as proof my father took after his father – whereas I don't think this was the same sort of thing at all.

When I'm finished, I'm amazed to see the glitter of tears in my mother's eyes. She nods slowly.

"Thank you, Rowan. I can see why my brothers felt obliged to keep their promise. On top of their oaths, they may have thought I'd be upset to know the truth."

"And you're not?"

"It's only what I'd expect of Arvan. Which is why I can't help but believe this far-fetched tale of yours. But I'm extremely glad to know my brothers weren't murderers. And" —her face suddenly blazes with enthusiasm— "it means there's no blood-guilt on me. It's like being set free!"

"To marry Ezra?"

"Well – yes. I could even do that!"

So now Kezzie and I are looking for Ezra. Well, mostly Kezzie. She seems to think that just by having sniffed the necklace he gave my mother, she's got enough of his scent in her nostrils to track him down. My mother's said if I just ask him to go and talk to her, she'll explain everything. (Of course, she could look for him herself. But I can see why she'd rather he has a bit of preparation. As well as Hawks – I've now realised – expecting other folk to act as messengers for them.)

Kezzie's taking me eastward. I suppose Ezra and his men have moved a bit downhill, with the North Camp packing up. People are bustling around on last-minute errands. A young man waves to me, and I can see it's Dirwan from the Shell tribe. Whom Anyanda thought so good-looking. I can see why, but I know he's keen on a young woman back home – he bought a gift for her only the day before last, when he came to my stall without any of his friends.

"Hi there, Rowan – and Kezzie," he says cheerfully. "Thanks for your help the other day. I reckon my girl will love that golden-brown neck warmer." Then he looks serious, and adds, "And I hear one of your aunts has gone to Spirit. My sympathies."

"Thanks."

"You know, if it had to happen, I reckon a temple festival's a good place for it. Like, the veils between the worlds are meant to be thinner here."

"That's a nice way to think of it. I'm actually looking for Ezra the Jewel-Trader."

"Oh – just met him round that clump of trees. He was talking to that Hawk who was done down in the archery contest." (Interesting – not only Kelvan who thought so, then.) "Seems quite decent – for a Hawk. Maybe him fancying other men helps him to be a bit less typical of them."

I'm surprised. "Did he tell you?"

Dirwan shrugs. "No. Just seems something I can tell about folk. Fine with me – like my mate says, leaves more girls for the rest of us." (And I bet a lot would prefer each other, or no one, to him; but he wouldn't believe it if you told him.) "I can tell other things on that sort of line," Dirwan continues. "Like when you were disguised as a man for the archery. I guessed you weren't, even before your hair fell down."

I remember my concerns about people who can sense male and female energies. "You didn't say, though."

"Because I hoped you'd beat that big-headed Beaver."

"I can understand that," I admit. "But Gerwas is all right really. And now he's married to my cousin!"

"Yeah – ran off two nights before the usual, didn't they? Seems as if some funny things have happened at this festival – and all to do with you, Rowan!"

"Not on purpose! Well…not all of them."

Dirwan grins. "Certainly kept things lively. I'll be glad to get back to the ship-building" —he did tell me he's a ship's carpenter – I think his friends are mostly in ship-building work too— "but I hope we'll meet again. In the meantime, the Goddess go with you!"

"And you," I say as we clasp hands. "And good luck with the gift!"

As Kezzie and I get round the trees, we see Ezra trying to bow, while Sparrow tries to take his hand. Then they must realise they've got different customs for signalling an agreement, because we see them laugh and slap each other on the shoulder. I guess they've been making travel plans.

"Rowan," Sparrow says quickly. "We're so sorry to hear about your aunt. What actually happened?"

"I will tell you. But Ezra – you've got to go to the West Camp now. My mother needs to talk to you."

"She does? But Rowan – what—?"

"Don't ask me anything! But I can tell you – it is for a very *good* reason!"

So Ezra rushes off as fast as a man his age can. Sparrow strolls westward with me and Kezzie while I tell him the whole tale. Apart from the bit I can't. I also tell him about what's happened with Kelvan, while Kezzie gives little growls of encouragement. Sparrow looks sympathetic.

"Kelvan has got a hasty temper," he admits. "Maybe he'll be sorry now for falling out with you."

"Maybe. But that wouldn't help about us wanting to do things with our lives that don't go together."

Sparrow doesn't have an answer to that. The three of us keep a friendly silence as we go downhill.

"Goodness," I say suddenly. "Isn't that my mother and Ezra in the middle of a big bunch of people?"

Sparrow shades his eyes. "Looks like them."

We all quicken our pace, until Sparrow and I are almost running beside Kezzie, who's just loping along. It definitely is them – but why the crowd?

"Rowan! Come and congratulate us!"

Ezra and my mother say this together, as the knot of folk around them unravels itself so Kezzie, Sparrow and I can get through. It looks like some Dragons who've been camped near us, and a few Beavers who've wandered up to see what's happening. So they haven't lost much time in making their announcement!

"We're going to have a quiet wedding tonight," my mother explains, "a blessing from the priesthood. Ezra doesn't want to go jumping bonfires – they don't in his country – and of course I'll be taking a turn to keep vigil for Jelize before the funeral. After that – we'll be ready to head for the coast!"

(And I have to say, they do look happy about it.)

"I've always wanted a daughter, Rowan," says Ezra. "And if you weren't planning to go to North Britain with Prince Kelvan, I'd be delighted if you could join us. Quite apart from all your mother and I owe you."

(This is embarrassing.)

"Uh – Kelvan and I have parted company."

My mother looks pleased to hear this. "I'm glad you've been sensible, Rowan. I did warn you against forming an alliance based on one week at a festival – at your age, I mean," she finishes hastily. "Although – you're still wearing his necklace! As well as some cheap bit of rubbish—"

"It's the Dreamstone, mother! I did explain about it!"

My mother now looks at it suspiciously. I guess she's not a great one for supernatural stuff, even when it's helped her, so I tuck it away. Now she's saying to Ezra, "Well – I'd best go and find Bram and Anya. And tell them our news."

Of course – they're not here. Maybe they're discussing plans for Jelize's funeral ceremony. They are her closest family from home, even if they don't know how close.

"Shouldn't I come with you?" asks Ezra.

"Well, of course. Normally. But under the circumstances…"

"Yes," Ezra agrees, "I'm sure they're very upset." (Well, I expect Bram is, anyway.) "And do assure them I won't expect a proper marriage night. I know you all have a vigil to keep. I just want us to be wed so you'll be able to journey with us the next day."

"Oh, I'll certainly be that," my mother says, flicking him a laughing glance; and I can't help comparing Ezra's attitude to wedding nights to Kelvan's – although maybe age lends patience. My mother adds, to me, "I take it, Rowan, you do want to come with us? I can ask Bram and Anya if they can take you and Kezzie in, now Anyanda's with the Beavers, if you want to go home."

I shake my head vigorously. "Of course I want to come with you! And" —as she presses against my leg— "so does Kezzie."

My mother smiles, taking this in good part. Maybe it helps that, at the moment, she's so happy – and grateful to me. Because she goes on to say, in a nice way, "Well, you've always wanted to see Egypt. Now you'll have your chance!"

And with that, she's off, leaving me and Ezra looking at each other.

"Rowan – could I look at that stone?"

Silently I fish it out again. Ezra doesn't take it from me, but he does turn it over in his palm. Then looks baffled.

"This looks like any cheap trinket to me. You see a heap of them any day in marketplaces and bazaars around the Middle Sea. Really they're just chips off real gemstones.

I think this one may be from a firestone – a garnet. The real thing is very popular in Egypt – reckoned to have special powers of protection.”

“And you believe that?”

“Well – I’m meant just to trust in God – Yahweh – and His angels. But I like to keep an open mind on the subject. Especially when it involves the beliefs of good customers.”

“But you’re saying something like this stone wouldn’t be reckoned to have special powers? Or be worth much to trade with?”

“Maybe trade four of them for half a loaf. Not like Kelvan’s fancy present.”

My hand flies to my neck. “I suppose I should give it back. But how can I? Kelvan’s gone.”

(And maybe part of me still wants to feel linked with him.)

“Just keep it under your tunic,” Ezra advises.

“And the Dreamstone?” (Which is how I now think of it.)

“Well – no one’s going to go robbing you for that. Unless they know it’s meant to have some special power.”

(I have to say, it does look pretty ordinary to me too.)

“Of course, you should be safe among my staff,” Ezra goes on. “And you’ll have your friend Sparrow with us, nice lad. His servants seem like decent men, too. I’ll be happy to have them all along with us for as far as they want to go. Then – well, I hope Sparrow finds what he’s looking for.”

“The husband? – Oh. Did you mean the fire-mountains?”

“Well, both. He did tell me about his first wish last night, when he and his friends performed in their North Camp. Think the mead had loosened his tongue a bit.”

“And you thought that was quite all right?”

Ezra pauses. Then he says, “Rowan – on my travels, I’ve seen how different places have different customs. As well as laws and religions. Different food, clothes, festivals – and, of course, marriage customs, although that may be partly due to varying weathers. So what I say is, just ask yourself if a custom's harming someone else. If not, live and let live."

I think about this. "That's good," I agree, "although if it was harming someone else – including other creatures, not just humans – I hope you'd do what you could to stop it."

Ezra smiles as I bend to stroke Kezzie, who's growling agreement. "I hope so too," he says. "Mind you, I don't know I'd be as active about it as I think you'd be!"

We all meet again for the final feast night. Ezra's wedding to my mother has gone off fine, although Uncle Bram looked a bit red-eyed – Aunt Anya more as if she was trying to stop herself from looking too cheerful. The priest who judged the archery contest, and the young priestess who gave a talk to the women that first night we were here, led the service. Probably the High Priestess is saving herself for the funeral. I can hardly believe that Jelize has gone to Spirit, but that's useful, because I can eat, drink and talk as usual. Sparrow comes to join us, with his two servants. These two are a bit hard to understand, though, because of their different-sounding speech, and use of some different words from us. I suppose the grander Hawks have more smoothed-out speech because they mix more with tribes from other parts of Britain – and that way they can boss the rest of us around better.

When everyone else is chatting among themselves, Sparrow turns to me and says, "I see you've put Kelvan's necklace away, Rowan."

"Oh – that. Well, Ezra told me to, because it's valuable. But that the Dreamstone wasn't. Only the High Priestess said I should hide that. So I've put them both under my tunic for now. And just keeping my shell out."

Sparrow looks thoughtful. "Would you mind if I touched this Dreamstone? Sometimes I can tell something about objects by their feel."

(A bit like me with Kelvan's brooch, I suppose.)

"Go ahead," I say, fishing it out and holding it towards him.

He takes it in one hand, and turns it over. Then shakes his head. "It doesn't feel like anything special to me," he says, a bit apologetically. "Maybe just a hint of lightning, like the air feels after a storm. It doesn't even feel especially old!"

I laugh. "Well, Ezra said you can get stones like this for almost nothing, anywhere around the Middle Sea. Maybe that's a good thing. But I'll tuck it back, just to be on the safe side!"

And now we've seen a bit of the great processions, my mother's insisting she and I go back to our shelter to get some rest, and have Anya call us two hours before dawn. As she says, we've had a tiring day. I don't expect, even with dear Kezzie warm beside me, and one of my mother's herbal drinks that's meant to make you drowsy, that I'll be able to sleep. But I do, plunging deeply into slumber, like falling off a cliff.

And I find I'm dreaming. Just everyday stuff at first, sitting at my loom while thinking up a new design. But now Jelize is with me! She's wearing a flowing skirt and top, in rainbow colours so bright you couldn't hope to create them in this world. Everything about her is sparkling, and she looks radiantly happy.

I drop my shuttle, and hold my hands out to her. "Jelize! You're alive! I thought you'd gone to Spirit."

Jelize takes my hands. Hers feel warm and cooling, all at once. And firm, but looking a bit see-through, like light. "Rowan – that's where you really are alive. More so than on your Earth."

(In the dream, I seem just to accept this.)

"Oh, Jelize! I'm so pleased for you. If you are so happy there. But I still need your advice – to guide me in this life."

"Well, Rowan, I did tell you there'd come a time when you'd have to manage on your own. But," she laughs, "I may be able to come back and help you, just occasionally. When you really need it."

With a swirl of her skirts, she's gone. And I'm wide awake, listening to my mother's soft snores and Kezzie's snuffling sounds. And you could say I'd just had a dream. But it feels like the most real thing that's ever happened to me in my life.

So, as Bram and the High Priestess take burning faggots to set the whole funeral pyre alight, high on the temple hill under an autumn sky streaked with pale yellow sunrise, I can't be too sad. There's a wonderfully big crowd too. All the Beavers here, as well as us Dragons – I suppose because of Anyanda and Gerwas – and more general well-wishers.

As the flames die down, I step backwards from the family, Kezzie still with me. I find a man's staring at me who looks a bit familiar under his hood. Then it comes to me – he's the Wolf outlaw. And it's plain he knows me.

CHAPTER 26

"Had to come and see her send-off, once I'd heard about it," he says, nodding his head towards the flames, "after what she did for us. Treated me like a real person, she did."

(Yes – I expect it was about that, not just the practical help.)

I can't help glancing around before asking, "Is it safe?"

The man smiles. Rather wolfishly. But Kezzie's beside me, and she seems quite friendlily disposed towards him.

"Well, of course you can," I say indignantly, "when you've come for a reason like paying your respects to my aunt."

(Which of course Jelize was, in the blood sense. I'm still a bit bemused by that one.)

"And we're hoping to turn respectable," he says rather wryly. "See, we've got some women among us. Oh, we never kept anyone against her will." (That's nice to know.) "But with some parties we've captured, there've been ones who want to find a husband – or get away from the ones they've already got."

"Yes, I can picture that," I admit. "So they're not happy with the outlaw life?"

He shakes his head sadly. "No. Most want us to turn

to peaceful trades – of course, we work the land to an extent now. And ask the Council of the North to recognise us as a proper tribe. In return for the usual tribute, of course."

"You know – if you want to get someone close to the Council on your side, try to get word to Kelvan."

"As in Prince Kelvan, the old king's grandson?"

"That's him. Or try his blood brother, Mart – Pine Marten. They're likely to see it makes sense." And I suppose they're still my friends – plus Mart often liked my ideas – so I add, "You can say Rowan the Weaver suggested it."

"Rowan the Weaver," he nods, as a mix of memorising and appreciating. He lifts one hand, keeping the one with missing fingers under cover. "Thanks – and go with the Goddess."

"You too – and good luck!"

Then he pauses, looking at my chest. But not in the personal way men do at Anyanda's. "Pretty," he says, nodding at Kelvan's gift, "but I take it you know the real power's in that stone you've got hidden underneath?"

My mouth opens wide. "How do you know?"

But he just grins, winks, and disappears among the crowd. And as it starts to break up, Kezzie's tugging at my skirt, with little growls. "Yes," I tell her, "I'll come back with you, and have breakfast. Then we can get ready for our travels."

"Me too?" I sense her asking. As she looks up at me, her dear face anxious, I realise she's concerned.

"Of course you too. Ezra and my mother know I wouldn't go without you. And they know you saved my life, so they've said they'll be honoured to have you with us."

Kezzie purrs happily. (To be honest, it was Ezra who said it, but my mother did join in with him; maybe some of his niceness will rub off on her – I'm sure that's something Jelize would have encouraged me to hope.)

As I'm bundling bits and pieces together, back at the camp, I feel a couple of hard, round, small objects in the bottom of my travelling bag. Of course – the love tokens! Well, Anyanda and I never found the need for them, and she'd given me hers for safekeeping anyway. What was it Jelize said? "Throw them in a bog, and maybe someone will find them in a few thousand years." So, with Kezzie for company, I slip off to that bathing pool with the muddy inlets. It's not an actual pool, but it will have to do.

With the help of Kezzie's paws, I'm managing to scoop really deeply into a muddy side wall. I've jumped in the water, first to wade, then to kneel (trying to tuck my skirt up a bit), as it's the only way I can do this. When I've finished, I look at the sky. Clouds are scudding by above branches that are already barer than when we were first here. I don't feel anything in particular. Not a sense of Jelize's presence – well, she warned me not to expect that. Nor any conclusion as to whether Kelvan's and my parting is for the best. Only a slight excitement at the new life which lies ahead of me, which I can't fully picture. I say a vague prayer for the love tokens, that they may come to light when the time is ripe – and for all of us to have a safe journey. And now I'd best return to camp.

Bram and Anya are outside our shelter, talking intently to my mother and Ezra, as we arrive. Which is good. Although my mother looks at my bedraggled skirt and wet boots, and remarks, "Did you step in a stream, Rowan?", she's not really interested where Kezzie and I have been. Which, I feel, isn't other folks' business. All the older ones do look pretty cheerful. Of course Ezra's happy. And Aunt Anya – maybe it's easier for her, someone who may have held her husband's heart being out of the way; or maybe she just likes the new, firm side to Uncle Bram, which he first showed on the night of Anyanda's wedding. You can see it now in the way he looks intently at my mother and, taking her hands, says:

"Sister Raven – I wish you joy in your marriage, and safety on your travels." He adds, glancing at Ezra, "I can tell you've chosen a good man."

My mother smiles at Bram. Her hair's unbound, so the wind's whipping it about and bringing a pink tinge to her usually pale cheeks. Ezra's looking at her more adoringly than ever.

"Well," she says, "I certainly found one great blessing in my first marriage. My new brother. Rowan and I will miss you, Bram."

"As we will you. And Kezzie, of course." Bram nods towards Kezzie, who rubs against him. He hugs me, and so does Aunt Anya. I hug them back, although Anya and I hold each other at a bit of a distance.

Bram and Ezra now move together, hands to each other's shoulders.

"And the Goddess go with you, Ezra ben Simeon, husband of my sister by marriage. Although if you prefer, I'll say Yahweh."

Ezra smiles. "Either is acceptable. With your good meaning behind it. I wish the same to you and your good lady. And remember, I hope to be back this way again. Maybe in another three years – so it's not goodbye for a lifetime!"

We're taking it in turns to have a quick midday meal while all the packing's finished. Of course, a lot of that involved Ezra and his men getting their wagons ready. Ezra says it doesn't matter if my mother and I only have a couple of changes of clothes to start – he can trade for more as we travel, as well as more weaving materials for me – and we'll find that as we get towards the hotter lands around the Middle Sea we'll need lighter clothing, even in winter. Kezzie thinks her fur will grow thinner, too. Sparrow's sitting with me, but now he says, "Think I'd better offer to lend Ezra a hand. Like my servants are doing. I don't want anyone thinking I'll be just a useless mouth to feed on the journey."

So I wave Sparrow off in Ezra's direction, and turn back to see if my mother wants any help from me. Although she may be getting settled in with her attendants. Ezra made sure he hired a couple of women to wait on her, and one for me, on the last full day of the festival. Some folk do go there partly to look for that sort of work, or to change employer. This took me a bit aback – after all, I've managed without anyone waiting on me for the first fourteen years of my life. But my mother took to it as if born to that life – which I suppose she was; well, once a Hawk...

I go past Sparrow's two men, who are talking earnestly to each other. And I can't help overhearing one of them say as I pass, "Bad news about young Kelvan."

"Yes," agrees the other. And despite his northern manner of speech, I can make him out quite clearly as he goes on, "and he really could swim like a fish. A fast fish. Last person I'd've thought would manage to get himself drowned!"

I stand still – feeling like one of those ice-mountains that are said to roam around seas to the far north. So I hear them go on.

"But that big river near here's pretty strange," the first man says. "The word is it can rise this time of year just like it was a sea at high tide."

"And lots of mudbanks – and currents he wouldn't know about." The other man shakes his head, almost as if he's starting to take gloomy relish in the news. And that makes me unfreeze.

"What's happened to Kelvan?" I yell, grabbing him by the arm.

"Mistress Rowan! We didn't see you," the first man says. He looks at Kezzie, who's started a low, rhythmic growling. And I don't know if he's picking up a message, or if it just makes him feel they need support. But either way, he says to his workmate, "Better get Ezra."

And Kezzie does stop growling as he goes to do so.

"Rowan – you've had a shock," Ezra's saying, his arm around my shoulders. "Do you want your mother – one of her herbal remedies?"

I shake my head. "Not at the moment."

(Because I can imagine her taking the attitude that if I'm so upset at this news, I should have appreciated Kelvan more when I had the chance. Because that's what I feel myself.)

"Well, I wouldn't worry too much about Prince Kelvan. If he's such a good swimmer as they all say, he's probably safe ashore. Just been swept up into some outlying place by your Big River's strange currents."

"I hope to the Goddess he has," I say, sniffing. "But then – he might have ended up somewhere else that's dangerous."

Ezra looks at me sympathetically, yet – however oddly – I could swear there's a twinkle in his eye. "I think, Rowan, you could do with meeting your attendant. I've done what you asked – hired someone your own sort of age, who can be more of a companion than someone who actually looks after you."

(That's true – I suppose I was hoping to get someone who'd sort of make up for Anyanda. Although, at the moment, I feel as if I could do with a bit of looking after.)

"Well – thank you."

"I'll take you to your wagon now," Ezra says. He takes one of my arms and almost pushes me along, while Kezzie tugs on my skirt as if encouraging me to go forward. They both seem to be placing a lot of faith in this attendant thing!

"Here," Ezra says, helping me up as he pulls a flap aside, "I'll leave you to introduce yourselves."

*

I blink in the dim light, seeing a tall, fair girl sitting on a bench with a rug beneath her.

"Hallo," I say, uncertainly. (I'm not sure how you greet attendants, but I don't want to sound as if I think I'm better than her.)

But as I take a step forward, Kezzie leaps on the girl in a joyful way. I recognise the long-fingered hands that come out to caress her – and the sharp-boned face – and I collapse on the opposite bench, gasping, "Kelvan!"

OUTRO

"You see, Rowan, it was your fault in the first place," Kelvan says.

"My fault! That you've turned up here as my attendant?"

"Well, you put the idea into my head – that disguising yourself as someone of the opposite sex is a good way to convince people you're that other person. As long as you do it right."

"Oh – from when I was Mab from the Mountains?" I say rather limply. "But" —I'm getting more excited now— "what about this tale of your drowning?"

"Oh, that's got about, has it? Good!"

"It's not good. I was" —may as well admit it— "very upset. So – what really happened?"

"I went swimming right enough. With Crow and Mart. Only they didn't go in far. We'd said we needed to freshen up before the journey. And the plan was they'd catch up with the rest with my clothes. Say they'd waited for me, but I must've got swept away on the currents."

"So you could have been," I say angrily. "The Big River's dangerous! Especially to anyone who doesn't know it!"

"Yes, but," Kelvan explains, "I had to show I'd really gone swimming. Even though I'd worked out there was a little gully I could hide in – I got Sparrow to put these clothes there – and take my harp for safekeeping."

"So you were all in on this plot?"

"I'd call it a plan. And of course we were – we're blood brothers! Mind, Mart needed a lot of persuasion. Scruples it might lead to him being named as future king."

"But doesn't he *want* to be?"

"Of course. That's why. But he'll be better at it than me. And as long as my grandfather thinks I'm dead, I'll be free to live my own life. With my harp. And, of course, you."

I can't help feeling warmed by the look in his blue eyes at this last remark. Kezzie purrs approvingly too. But still – fancy giving up the chance of ruling a kingdom without even a backward glance! How very Hawk: or maybe just very, very Kelvan.

"I briefed Crow and Mart what to say to my mother, too. Tell her about it in confidence – as if they thought my grandfather might want it kept a secret until he knew – but make sure her most gossip-given servant was within earshot."

"Poor Eleri!"

"Oh, she knew the truth already. Who d'you think helped me get these clothes? And the female plaits?" He adds, "I'm still from North Britain, of course – goes with my height. Extra fair, because my father was a shipwrecked sea-rover. My name's Galina. And I'm quite shy, so I don't talk much or look folk in the eye."

(That makes sense. But Kelvan seems to be taking this very seriously. I've heard of countries where people act out whole stories in a valley or round a campfire. I can see Kelvan would be good at that – much better than I would be. Especially if he could play his harp and sing too.)

"All right," I say cautiously. "I'm happy this has Eleri's blessing. But how *many* people know about your – uh – plan?" It suddenly hits me. "Ezra – he does!"

"Well, yes. I didn't think I could deceive him. And I didn't want to. But of course, if I get found out, it was something I hatched out on my own."

"That sounds fair. But I hope you won't be!"

"Yes – I'm a bit worried about my disguise. Because when I met Sparrow after the final feast night, and we were walking towards Ezra's folk, we did bump into two Shell men – those same ones who tried to attack us."

"Goodness! Did you have any trouble with them?"

Kelvan smiles. "Not in that way! The drunker one tried to kiss me. Even though I might've been Sparrow's girl. I was going to punch him, but Sparrow hissed at me– 'just slap' – and then his mate dragged him away – saying to us, 'He doesn't realise just how much he's wasting his time.'"

"Oh, that'll've been Dirwan. He can sense things about male and female energies. Maybe he thought you were Sparrow's boyfriend! Anyway, it's not how you looked – or the other one wouldn't have been keen!"

"Well, I'm only going to act as your attendant until we're across the Shallow Sea. Then I'll turn into a baggage handler. Ezra's happier for me to be with the other men until we're a long way from Britain – and you and I can be properly married. We've not told your mother, either. Ezra doesn't think it's fair on her until there's enough distance between us and Britain for it not to alarm her."

(I don't think my mother's the easily alarmed sort. But I'm not sure where her loyalties would lie, so I reckon that's a good decision.)

Kelvan moves to the same bench as me, Kezzie coming to sit by both our sets of feet.

"I'm glad, Rowan," he says teasingly as he fingers my necklace, "to see that you're still wearing my heart."

"Oh – yes. Although Ezra said I should wear it under

my tunic. Because it's pretty valuable."

"So did he give you this piece of rubbish to wear as a cover for it?" Kelvan asks, flicking out the Dreamstone with one of his long fingers. "Or is it a gift from one of your Shell friends?"

My hand goes to it instinctively. "Oh – of course. You don't know about the Dreamstone."

So I tell him.

Kelvan listens attentively to the whole story, while Kezzie goes to sleep on our feet. Even to the bit about the High Priestess really being Jelize's mother. He's the one person I feel able to tell, and that I trust to tell. Actually, he doesn't seem too interested in that bit. Whereas he wasn't very happy about my going in for spirit travel, muttering I was a fine one to tell other people off for doing anything that could be a bit dangerous.

After I've finished, he picks the Dreamstone up again, holding it between thumb and fingers.

"So – this may not look much, but it could be pretty powerful. Can you make it do anything else?"

"I don't think I can *make* it do anything, even if I wanted to. Actually – I don't totally understand how it works. First Ezra said it was practically worthless for trading with. Then Sparrow said it didn't have any special feel to him, except a bit crackly – like the air after a storm. But the wolf-man – that's an outlaw I made friends with, who came to Jelize's funeral – he could tell there was something special about it, even when it was under my tunic."

Kelvan drops the stone, and looks thoughtful. "Maybe it's not this Dreamstone thing in itself. Maybe it's just your tool – like me with my harp. Because I reckon that, even more than the weaving, you've got a gift for making things happen – causing changes."

I think of what Dirwan said about me. "Maybe. I hope they're good ones, then. And I'd only want to use it for something important. I don't want to go around having visions all the time! I'm glad you don't mind the idea of marrying someone who can do that, though. I reckon lots of men might find it a bit scary."

"No, I think it's quite exciting…" Kelvan grins suddenly, and there's a dancing light in his eyes. "Actually – I think all this is. I mean – chance to travel! You're right about that being a good thing. And maybe in Egypt I'll have a chance to meet this person Ezra said was trying to invent a bag-pipe, too. And meet these female harpists."

"Ezra wants to visit his parents first, mind. Folk who live their side of the Middle Sea can be quite long-lived – maybe it's their weather and food. Or the wine. Anyway, he's also keen to catch up with this rich cousin of his, called Jacob, so that bit might not be very exciting."

"Rowan – I'm looking forward to going anywhere with you. A harpist, a lynx and a dreamweaver on the road together. Anything might happen!"

"Yes – when you put it like that," I agree, "I think it might!"